The Naphil's Kiss

Simone Beaudelaire

Published 2021 by Next Chapter
Cover art by Cover Mint
Back cover texture by David M. Schrader, used under license from Shutterstock.com

Acknowledgments

I would like to thank my beta readers: Guy Bailey, T. Jackson King, Sandra Martinez, Ch'kara Silverwolf, Edwin Stark and Lisa Williamson

For Charles, because inspiration comes from many different places. Thank you.

Prologue

The Nephilim were on the earth in those days- and also afterward- when the sons of God went to the daughters of men and had children by them. They were heroes of old, men of great renown.

Genesis 6: 4

And to this day, they remain; the Nephilim. Half human, half angel. They hide in the light – eternal, chaste, and beautiful. They protect the children of men from the Succubi, daughters of Lilith. Dangerous demonesses who prey on men, leaving them worse than dead.

Until the day one Naphil, Lucien, first encountered the Succubus Sarahi. That day a creature of darkness, sick of the shadows, dared lift her face towards heaven and discovered something she never dreamed she would find... love.

Part I

Chapter 1

Rome 78 AD

Sarahi made her slow, sinuous way down the cobbled streets of Rome, between the heavily-columned white marble buildings, heading for the temple of Venus. Hunger snarled in her belly. It had been far too long since she had eaten – months – but she'd been unable to rid herself of the image of Alexander dying in her arms, drained of his life force by her insatiable hunger. *Poor man. He was so beautiful, so strong. A warrior in the bedroom and on the field of battle.*

It's so unfair that I can never keep a man, only use him until I suck him dry. My nourishment is my lover's downfall. This is my only alternative, and I hate this more. Prostitution. Trading one man for another until I'm sated. Disgusting. But if she went much longer without feeding, she risked losing control, and that would be worst of all. She could drain a man to his destruction in a single feeding.

Bah, being a demoness is not at all what people think. I have so little power. Oh, I can shrink down to a tiny size, and incite people to lust, but what good are those attributes? What use? I live like an animal, mating and feeding. And for me, they are one.

As she approached the temple, she could feel the sexual energy rising, could taste it. Inside, behind the perfectly rectangular palisade of fluted columns, under the shallow peak of the roof, powerful men exchanged their hard-earned coins for a night with one of the beautiful women employed in honoring the goddess of love. They had no idea how many of those women were Succubi. *It's an easy meal. No need to hunt. The prey comes right to your hand.*

"Hmm." A handsome young man eyed her. "Very pretty."

Sarahi pinned him with a gimlet stare and pulled the cerulean shawl closer over her scarlet hair. It was the best she could do. She could not disguise her milk-pale skin or her glowing green eyes. At least she could hide the hair.

But why am I hiding? I could go with that young man right now and feed. He's agreeable. I can feel it, can feel the lust radiating off him. She frowned. *I don't want that. Lilith take it, I don't want him. I don't want anyone. I want to be left alone.*

Her belly cramped with hunger and she took another look at the back of the young man as he hurried away from her. *If I call him, he will come.* She opened her mouth, letting the slightly bisected tip of her tongue protrude, and inhaled... tasted...

What is that aroma in the air, that celestial fragrance? Like a man, but the best kind of man. Freshly washed but wearing no perfumes to disguise his natural scent. Strong. Sweet. Delicious. What is the source? It teased her. She turned.

A man was walking down the street.

There's nothing unusual about it, really, so why can I not stop staring? Hundreds, perhaps thousands of men each day walked the path to and from the Senate, the temple, and the bathhouses. *There's nothing remarkable about this man who seems to be heading in the same direction as I am.*

Well, actually there is something unusual about him. He's incredibly tall. Also dark. His tightly-shorn curls gleamed blacker than the dusk. His back was to her, but through his white robe, she could see his fine, muscular physique. Her mouth watered at the sight of him. *Oh, I can just see how delicious his energy would taste. I can taste the faintest morsel of it now.*

Sarahi wiped her hand over the corner of her mouth and hurried after him. *If he's heading to the temple now, this is my lucky day. I wouldn't mind making a meal of this one.*

Sure enough, he strode directly there, but instead of entering, he lingered outside the door. He turned to face the street and Sarahi's breath caught. *Has there ever been such a beautiful face? Firm jaw, eyes like polished ebony, strong broad nose, full sensual mouth. He was made to be loved.* She wanted him more than ever.

As men approached the entrance, he touched them on the arm. Those full lips twisted into words she couldn't make out. No one turned his way, but everyone he touched paused. Some turned away and hurried down the street. Others steeled themselves and entered.

They can't see him. He touches them, talks to them, but they have no idea he's there.

Interesting that I can see him. She approached. He turned those burning, midnight eyes on her.

"Come no closer, Succubus," he intoned, his voice strong and deep. She shivered at the sound of it. Her face curving into a sensuous smile, she walked towards him, deliberately crowding into his space and letting him smell her perfumed, womanly sweetness. His nostrils flared.

"How did you know what I am?" she asked, drawing her voice out long and slow.

His Adam's apple bobbed. "Of course, I know what you are, slut. Do *you* know what *I* am?

"Oh, for Lilith's sake," she hissed, suddenly furious. "Naphil. I should have guessed." *My delicious meal is a half-angel sworn to celibacy.* Now Sarahi felt like swearing.

"You should have *known*, little one," he chided.

"I've never seen a Naphil before." *Goddesses, but he's beautiful, and what is that expression... amusement?*

His full lips twisted into a wry parody of a smile. "Then you are poorly trained. You'll not be going in there tonight."

"What difference does it make?" She demanded, arms akimbo. "Those men are going in to bed a woman. They will walk out unharmed. Why deny me admittance?"

"It is my duty." He paused, his proud expression turning considering, and gestured with a twist of his head toward the columns flanking the entrance. "Do you *want* to be there?"

Sarahi took a risk. "No." She looked directly into his eyes. "But you might as soon reason with the lion not to eat the antelope. He hungers, and he cannot stop himself." She sighed.

He narrowed his eyes. "What do you mean?"

She regarded him, confused. "You say you are trained to know us. Surely you must know *why* we do what we do."

"Yes. To gain power. To threaten Heaven." He gestured with one broad hand.

She laughed, the sound bitter to her own ears. "No, Sir Naphil, you are misinformed. We seduce men, not to gain control of them, but to feed. The energy produced by the act of copulation is our only source of nourishment."

The realization twisted his face. "You feed on men?" He drew back from her in disgust.

Sarahi stepped forward again, silently pleading with him to understand. "It is in my nature to do so, and yet..."

He drew up to his full, towering height, his shadow blocking out the evening sun, and raised on hand to halt her progress. "Yet?" he demanded.

She looked up at him through lowered eyelashes. "Yet I would prefer to eat bread and drink wine like everyone else. This is a cursed existence."

He pondered. "What if you fed on only one; a husband or lover?"

Sarahi's breath caught. *Why do you care, angel? Why do you ask questions?* She could feel her lip trembling. "No man would survive it long. A few months at most. My last..." she trailed off and turned away.

A warm hand closed on her shoulder. Her gown was held shut by a clip, and around it, his fingers touched her bare skin. "I am sorry. I did not realize."

She turned back to face him, her eyes swimming. "Do not judge what you don't understand, Naphil. Your kind doesn't know everything about mine."

"Lucien." No longer disapproving, his tender tone flowed over her like honey, warm and sweet. It captured her, and so she struggled to understand his meaning.

"What?" Sarahi blinked away the drugging lure of his unconscious sensuality.

"My name is Lucien," he repeated.

She smiled. "How apt. Well, Lucien, I haven't fed in ages. If I don't eat soon, I'm likely to lose control, and then you'll have to slay me." Biting her lip in a seductive gesture, she added in a pseudo-innocent voice, "Do you wish to slay me, light bearer?"

He considered her in silence for an endless moment, and then said, "No, Succubus. I do not wish to slay you."

A true smile curved her lips, and she thrilled to see him react to it, if only by the flaring of his nostrils. "I am called Sarahi."

Lucien lowered his chin in acknowledgment. "I will remember. I do apologize for... everything."

"Accepted." Hostility dispersed, the longing to possess, or at least to taste, this glorious creature threatened to overwhelm her. She swallowed. *Don't be a demoness now, woman. He's a creature of the light.* But desire overcame sense, urging her aching, needy body in his direction. "Please go elsewhere. Save innocent victims." She bit her lip again, this time in true consternation. At last, she admitted, "I don't want to waste my strength trying to do the impossible."

"Which would be what?" he demanded, demonstrating his innocence.

"Feed on you," she informed him bluntly.

He scoffed. "You couldn't."

Such confidence. I doubt you're as strong as you think you are, sir Naphil. She released a thin thread of enticement, and his eyes widened. When she spoke, her sultry desire oozed from her voice. "Only if I could seduce you. But if I could..." She twirled a strand of hair around her fingertip.

"Then?" The bobbing of his Adam's apple in the ebony column of his throat contradicted his challenging tone.

"Then I think you'd make the tastiest meal I've ever eaten." She approached, pressing her body against his and sliding her arms around his neck. Pulling his head down, she kissed him. To her amazement, he didn't resist. She pulled him closer, sliding her tongue along the seam of his lips before dipping inside.

He was even more delicious than she had imagined, especially as desire began to rise within him. Her hunger eased, she became aware of a new emptiness, one she hadn't felt in what seemed like ages. *I want him, but as more than just nourishment.*

She ran her fingertips down his arms and guided his hands to her slender waist before reaching up to embrace him again.

In a matter of moments, her aching belly had filled to capacity. She realized with a start that she no longer needed to feed. *My hunger is satisfied, and all from just a kiss.*

She released his mouth, guilt warring with purring satisfaction. "Go, Lucien. Leave this place. You've made vows. I'll not be the one to tempt you into breaking them. Go."

He stared at her in stunned disbelief for the space of several heartbeats, and then he disappeared as though he'd never been there at all.

Sarahi drew in a shaky breath and licked her lips, tasting the honey-sweet residue of his desire. *How can I feed on another after that? It would be like eating ashes.*

A pleasing thought occurred to the Succubus. *Perhaps it's not necessary to complete a sex act in order to feed. Perhaps I can feed on unconsummated lust, or even on that of others. Be nearby, mop up a little of the excess energy, and spare myself the humiliation.*

How ironic to bless the day I met my enemy face to face.

Chapter 2

Versailles, France, 1660

Sarahi examined the sumptuous bedroom in which she was hiding. Though she rarely concerned herself with the fate of mortals, even she had to admit this wasteful luxury seemed wrong. *Ragged peasants succumb to disease in the streets, their children starve, yet the king and his court dare to flaunt their excesses in such a fashion. It's disgusting.* Of course, with all the leisure time these corpulent noblemen and women enjoyed, indulging in lustful interludes provided a common means of diversion from the boredom of extreme wealth.

A key clicked softly in a lock, followed by a feminine giggle. Sarahi quickly shrank down to the size of a mouse and hid among the assortment of colored glass perfume bottles littering the boudoir table below a huge gilded mirror. She glanced at the bed. Royal blue silk hung from towering wooden posts carved with intricate designs. A fold in the luxurious blue and gold brocade bedding revealed gleaming white linens.

A giggling matron in her middle thirties, her head covered in a powdered wig of astonishing height, pulled a much younger man into the room and locked the door. He had his face buried in the cleavage revealed by the low front of her gown. She dragged him to the bed.

"Déshabillez-vous," he told her, formal even in such an intimate setting.

"Fais-le toi-même," she shot back, turning so he could unlace her gown. He began eagerly pulling at the strings.

Sarahi drank in their desire. *Ahhh, that's better. Of all the choices available, voyeur is best. They're going to do this anyway,* she rationalized. *What difference does it make if I take a little taste? They will attribute their fatigue to satiation and recover fully by tomorrow.*

A shadow crossed in front of the window, and Sarahi looked up sharply. The couple, still struggling with the lacings of the woman's cumbersome gown, did not react at all.

Naphil...I have to get out of here... But then Sarahi detected the telltale fragrance, even masked as it was by the sweat of the unwashed couple finally embracing naked on the bed.

"Succubus, I know you're here. Show yourself!"

Oh, that voice... just the sound of it is more satisfying than anything happening on the other side of the room. Cautiously, she stepped out from between the bottles, to the edge of the table.

"Lucien," she called softly. Over the centuries, they had found each other often, and while she could feel the beautiful half-angel's desire spark every time he saw her, he remained stubbornly faithful to his vow of celibacy. That shattering kiss they'd shared in Rome had never been repeated, much to Sarahi's disappointment.

"You," he growled.

"Are you going to slay me this time?" she teased.

"Are you harming anyone?"

"Never," she vowed. "Just having a bit of lunch, courtesy of our friends over there. You didn't really think you would be able to dissuade them, did you? They've been lusting after each other for weeks."

"With your help," he reminded her, his tone an accusation.

She shrugged, her flirtatious manner firmly in place. *I do love teasing him...I think he might love it too. Otherwise, why would he stay to banter?* "I may have whispered a few suggestions in his ear, but, Lucien, if he didn't want her, it wouldn't have mattered. Just as you cannot stop someone who is truly determined, I cannot create desire where none exists. You and I are two sides of the same coin, love. We can only enhance what is already there."

He gave her an angry look, his onyx eyes flashing in the dark skin of his beautiful face.

"Don't, Lucien. If you dislike it so much, why don't you feed me yourself?" She felt her eyes glowing hot as she voiced her greatest wish aloud.

His face registered surprise at her boldness, followed by longing, and then rage. "Why? I have no desire to be one of your legion of lovers."

Her cheeks burned as the accusation struck her to the center of her heart. *Do you think I wanted to live that way? I had no choice.* Stung, she argued back, "I have no lovers. No legion. Not even one. This is the only way I feed, now. It's so much better this way."

"Then why..."

Though she didn't know if he could see the lust in her eyes, when she had shrunk herself to the size of a mouse, she let it smolder anyway. "Oh, my dearest angel, surely you must know how I desire you. Only you, Lucien."

For the most fleeting of moments, desire flared in his eyes, but he quickly suppressed it. His back teeth ground together. "I have sworn vows."

"I know you have. One of them was to kill any Succubus on sight, was it not? How well have you kept that vow?" She tilted her head to one side.

He swallowed hard but said nothing. She stepped off the edge of the table. His big hand shot out and caught her as she fell, just as she had hoped he would.

"Don't tempt me, Sarahi. No good can come of it." He lifted her up close to his face.

"I disagree, Lucien. Every good can come of it." She trailed tiny fingertips along his palm, glorying in the conflicted desire that raged across his face.

"I won't feed you," he insisted stubbornly.

She wrapped her body around his finger, letting him feel her lush curves beneath her thin, ruby-colored dress. She kissed his fingertip. "You already have," she teased, but it was the wrong thing to say. Snarling, he set her back on the table and disappeared.

Sarahi smiled ruefully as the couple on the bed ground their bodies together. Their lust tasted terrible after the clean sweetness of Lucien. A moment later, she disappeared as well.

Chapter 3

New York, 1923

Sarahi regarded herself in the full-length mirror and adjusted her dress, so the black lace settled even lower on her ample bosom, creating a rather ridiculous amount of cleavage. Her victim would not be able to see her, so it didn't matter whether she looked her best or not, but she wanted to be successful, and when she looked sexy, she felt sexy. *I'm ravenous tonight, but this party in the penthouse of a luxury apartment building will be an easy place to feed.* For three hours, she had followed her lusty victim, Tom, through a haze of alcohol, music, and women in short, fringed skirts, whispering suggestions in his ear. *Soon it will be time to move in for the kill... figuratively speaking of course.* In the morning, he'd have a monster of a hangover, but as drunk as he was, he likely wouldn't expect anything different.

She glanced around the room. In a city with so little available space, owning an extra bedroom to use as a dressing room was a sure sign of extreme wealth. Only a red velvet chaise and a carved wardrobe took up space on the floor. *Tom must be doing quite well.* Sarahi's stomach rumbled. *Time to go get a snack.*

Tossing her burgundy hair over her shoulder, she gave herself one last look, and then, satisfied with her appearance, she flashed to a spot on her victim's left shoulder. Sarahi smirked to see Lucien, in all his midnight beauty, on the right. The lovely angel man had resisted her a long time, but he was wavering. She could feel it. *Perhaps I can feed more directly tonight. I only want to when he's here.*

A wicked smile curled her lips upwards. She turned her attention to her victim. *Curly brown hair and pretty blue eyes, as well as far too much money for his own good.* She scanned the room. The polished floor gleamed, as did the satin bedding on which a woozy-looking woman reclined, looking up with unfocused eyes. From outside, the sounds of the party continued unabated.

He's delicious and already slightly drunk, which will make my job so much easier. The desire radiating from him started to fill her empty belly immediately. She watched his mouth descend again towards the pretty and intoxicated blond he had already kissed so deeply, his hands lifting the skirt of her short, fringed dress.

"Do it," she purred in his ear. Inside his head, her seductive voice sounded like his own, so he would not realize he was being tempted by an evil creature like herself. "Take her," Sarahi continued. "You know she wants it. She came here to get this from you, and she's not really that drunk. She's only had two gin fizzes... maybe three. No more than three. She knows what she desires."

She sensed him considering and pressed. "Just think how it would feel... hmm soooo good." Her voice became sticky and slow, like molasses, and then she shimmied over to the side of his head. Her little pink tongue snaked out, licking the ear almost as big as she was. He shivered as though he could feel it. *He's hooked now, and my hunger is satisfied. Time to take a chance.*

Sarahi sidled around his neck, trailing her fingers along his sensitive hairline, and addressed Lucien directly. "He's all yours. Choose, Lucien. Do you waste your time trying save the guilty from themselves, or do you come with me? Please me, and you can have all this." She trailed her fingertips across her cleavage, delighted to see the angel's eyes following her movements. "Don't disappoint me."

Then she disappeared.

Sarahi flashed herself back to the still-empty dressing room and waited. She had invited him before, but he had never come. *Maybe tonight will be different.*

She stretched out on a red velvet chaise, arms behind her head, and waited. Over the centuries it had become easier to incite lust and feed from it, but after all this time, she could never let go of what she really wanted; the Naphil Lucien in her bed. She was nearly frantic with it.

His scent wafted across her nostrils. Her nipples hardened painfully, and she felt herself growing wet.

"Sarahi?"

"Lucien."

"What did you want, Succubus?" His voice sounded weary.

Opting for honesty instead of seduction, Sarahi spoke bluntly. "You know what I want. I told you in Versailles, over four hundred years ago. Nothing has changed. I want you."

"Why?" he demanded.

"Who can say? I certainly can't explain it."

"I don't want to feed you," he pleaded.

She lowered her lashes, acknowledging the legitimacy of his feelings. "I can't help that. It's what I am. But that's not why I want you."

"Then why?" he demanded again.

You know, Lucien, if you dared admit it to yourself. "Come over here, my love, and find out."

He approached cautiously and knelt on the floor beside her.

She reached out her hand and trailed dainty fingers over the coarse curls on his head. "Have you forgotten how it was in Rome? I've never had a kiss like that."

His full lips twisted into a parody of a smile. "Sarahi, I've never had a kiss other than that."

She couldn't help smiling in return, and it seemed to draw him to her like a static charge. As though against his will, his arms slipped around her waist and he lowered his mouth to hers, taking the lead as though he had the experience of all his centuries of existence behind him. It was the hottest kiss she'd ever had, far eclipsing that long-ago day in Rome.

It seemed he'd never forgotten that day either, the day he'd first encountered temptation. Then, she'd tasted his mouth. Now he returned the favor, plunging his tongue past those naturally red lips.

She moaned at the honey-sweet flavor of him, snaking her arms around the bulky thickness of his shoulders to pull him even closer. He climbed onto the chaise, straddling her body and pressing her into the soft upholstery. She wrapped her legs around his waist. Their bodies aligned completely.

She hadn't been sure what kind of sex organs a Naphil might have, but the bulge grinding against her felt normal, apart from the lovely size of it. *This is going to be spectacular, worth all the centuries I've waited.* She hummed into his mouth.

"Touch me, my angel," she murmured when he released her mouth to drag air into his lungs. She took his hand from behind her back and guided it to one of her full breasts, tugging down the fabric to expose it.

For a moment, he caressed her there, and the sight of his ebony skin against her gleaming white flesh made her catch her breath. *Such a beautiful contrast.*

And then he stopped. "I... Sarahi, I can't... No." He rose from the chaise.

"Lucien, please. Don't go," she begged. *No! Not now.*

"I swore a vow," he reminded her, desperate passion and stubborn obedience warring in his features.

"Who would know?" she asked. "It could be our secret." *Goodness knows I'm no more allowed than he is, but he's worth every risk.*

"*He* would," Lucien answered, cryptic as usual.

"God?"

"The head of the elder council, our governing body. He would know."

"Is he omniscient?" Sarahi sat partially upright, meeting Lucien's dark-eyed gaze with a challenging stare of her own.

"No, but how could I keep it from him?"

"You could if you tried."

"No, Sarahi. I can't. I... I'm sorry." And he vanished from the room as though he had never been there.

Sarahi turned over on the chaise and wept into the scarlet upholstery, her belly full, but her heart breaking.

Chapter 4

Los Angeles, 1978

Sarahi sat at a table in the semi-dark nightclub. A disco ball hanging from the ceiling threw dizzying lights over the couples on the dance floor. She sipped a martini while her companions made out beside her. Linda – a black woman with an enormous afro, dressed in a white jumpsuit that clung to her every curve – had arrived already under the influence. Guillermo, a skinny Hispanic man with a pencil-thin mustache, who wore a powder blue leisure suit, had snorted a line the moment he sat down at the table. Now they were both so high it didn't matter to them in the slightest whom they were groping.

These two are a bit disgusting. Wish I could leave. Come on, stomach... come on. Somehow the display of drug-addled lust lacked potency.

She tugged on the neckline of her backless metallic silver top. The chains that held it across the back tickled her skin. *It's hot in this room, and not just with passion.* Her polyester pants clung to her sweaty thighs. Easy pickings came at a price.

At last, the sharpest edge of her hunger eased. She rose, no longer desiring a full feeding, and headed for the door.

The man looked up. "Where are you getting off to, Sarah?"

"I'm going home," she told him. "I've had enough for tonight."

"Don't go," Linda urged. "Stay. We have some gooood coke." She waved a tiny glass bottle in Sarahi's direction. "You can have some."

Sarahi shuddered. *I do not want any cocaine.* "No, thank you."

Guillermo grabbed her arm.

"Let me go," she told him softly. She could throw him off easily enough, but that would raise questions she couldn't afford to answer. She tugged gently, hoping to dislodge his clinging hand.

"Don't hurry off," he said. "Stay."

"Let me go, Guillermo, or I'll hurt you," she told him. He laughed.

Guillermo's condescending chuckle turned to a gasp of disbelief as a huge dark hand clamped down on his arm, forcing him to release her.

"She said she was leaving," a deep, rumbling voice said behind her.

Oh Lilith, that voice. Sarahi closed her eyes and then opened them, turning to look at the familiar face she hadn't seen in over fifty years. "Lucien!"

"Sarah, do you know this dude?" Linda demanded, eyeing Lucien with interest.

"Yes." No more needed to be said.

"Come with me." Lucien extended his hand to Sarahi. She took it without hesitation, following him out of the building to the street.

Outside, heat shimmered above the asphalt, but compared to the stuffy, sweltering club, it felt almost refreshing. Neither heat could match the inferno of Sarahi's desire. She threw her arms around Lucien and pulled him down into a wild kiss, unable to control herself.

He kissed her back for long moments, cradling her in his arms as he made love to her mouth. Then he slowly lifted his head.

"Where have you been?" she asked him.

"Avoiding you." His plump lips twisted.

"Why?"

"I had to. I've sworn..."

"I know." She laid a palm on his cheek. "But, then, Lucien, why are you here?"

"I couldn't...I..." He closed his eyes. "I couldn't stay away. How do you draw me to you, Sarahi?"

She laughed bitterly, without humor. "Do I have to tell you? Surely you know, you feel it too."

"I feel something I don't understand," he admitted, then his confusion gave way to anger. "How do you do this to me? Do you use your powers to make me feel this way?"

Sarahi refused to take offense. "No, Lucien. I can't create desire from nothing. It comes from you, and I've done nothing to enhance it."

"Then what is it?"

She smiled, wistful and sad. "It's simple, my angel. It's love. I love you, and you love me too. And you want me. Don't deny it."

"I can't deny it any longer." He closed his eyes. When he opened them, the obsidian depths glowed with a passion that reflected all she felt.

She cupped his cheek in her hand, letting centuries of adoration and longing express themselves on her face, showing him he was not feeling this alone. "Then come with me, Lucien. Come away. Be with me."

He looked at her doubtfully, desire warring with uncertainty.

Sarahi felt stung. *As long as I've waited for him... but how could he know?* "Do you still think I do this with anyone? Lucien, do you know how long it's been since I invited a man to my bed?"

He shook his head.

"The last man who made love to me was Alexander. I was mourning his death the day we met in Rome. It's been almost two thousand years."

She held out her hand, waiting, holding her breath. Slowly, hesitantly, he placed his huge dark hand inside the whiteness of her little palm. Their fingers laced together. In a blink, Los Angeles disappeared.

They rematerialized standing on a little patch of blasted and withered scrub. In front of them, an endless stretch of rust-colored sand gave way to low foothills. The Mojave Desert. And just to the right, a travel trailer sat in the partial shade of a shriveled little tree.

"Where are we?" he asked.

"This is my place," Sarahi explained. "I come here to be alone."

She led him up the clanking metal steps, through a cheap screen door, which banged noisily against the siding. Tugging his hand, she led him straight to the back, where the built-in bed had been covered with a thin blanket the color of the desert sand outside. She tossed it aside to reveal cotton sheets of sunset orange.

Sarahi reached for the edge of her top, but Lucien grasped her hand gently. She looked at him, a question in her eyes.

"Let me." His words, dark with passion, brought a true smile to her lips. When he lifted her garment over her head, she raised her arms to help, wanting nothing more than to be close to him.

Under a scrap of fabric like that, she could not wear a bra. At the sight of Sarahi's naked breasts, Lucien to sucked in an unsteady breath. *That's right, touch me,* she urged silently. He reached out slowly and cupped one full globe in his dark hand.

"So beautiful," he told her. She could see the question in his eyes and gently showed him how to caress her, guiding his fingers to her nipple. Her breath caught as he fondled the distended nub. *I forgot how sharp the pleasure could be.*

"Oh, Lucien," she moaned, "that feels so good." She let him play with her for a few tantalizing seconds, before she took a step back and offered him a warm smile. As he watched, she slowly stripped off her pants and lowered herself onto the bed. She looked into his eyes and saw it; *there will no going back.* The truth of what was to come added to the song coursing through her body. She felt him in her core and her skin, in her blood and her bones. She felt his energy taking possession of her being, as if he were already inside her.

He undressed with aching slowness, revealing the body she'd hungered to taste for untold centuries, and climbed onto the bed beside her, pulling her into his arms.

"Hmm," she sighed against his mouth as he pressed her close to him. "I love you, Lucien."

"I love you, Sarahi."

"Touch me again." She rolled to her back and urged his head down to her breast, feeling the coarse thickness of his close-cropped curls. His mouth opened around her nipple with no further urging, and he sucked it in, lashing the tender peak with his tongue. She writhed with pleasure.

While he tended first one aching breast and then the other, she stroked her hand down the hard, dark muscles of his chest, reaching lower until she found what she wanted. Wrapping her fingers around his huge, thick erection, she stroked him, gently at first, and then with increasing speed and pressure.

Lucien groaned. "Stop, love."

"Why?"

"It's too much."

"Oh..." *I forgot he's never made love before.* This new stimulation would bring him to culmination quickly if she wasn't careful. *Another time, once he's learned the ways of loving better, I can caress and fondle him. But for now, it's time to bring centuries of longing to an end.* She opened her thighs, slipping them to the outside of his, and urged him over her, loving the weight of his massive body pressing her into the bed.

She took hold of that heavy sex again and guided him to the long-ignored opening of her body.

"Take me, Lucien," she urged. He arched his hips slowly, and Sarahi cried out with joy as he filled her as no one ever had before. The pressure of his penetration sufficed to ignite an orgasm the likes of which she had never imagined, and she wept with pleasure at its strength.

The ecstatic clenching of her internal muscles brought Lucien to the first climax of his entire existence. He groaned at the unexpected sensation and lowered his mouth to hers for a long and perfect kiss.

Chapter 5

The Mojave Desert 1978

Sarahi sat on a metal folding chair outside her travel trailer. Hunger gnawed furiously at her belly. *This is insane. I should be able to go many weeks between feedings, even months if necessary. But now, after only six weeks, I feel as though starvation is setting in.*

Maybe my reserves are low because of grief. She'd never had such a beautiful night as the one she had spent with Lucien, but when she woke in the morning he'd been gone, his honey-sweet love energy draped over her body like a blanket, but his powerful presence no longer beside her in the bed.

She'd grieved that desertion like she hadn't grieved in centuries, not since Alexander. *My poor darling. He loved me with a passion unequaled among human men – my warrior, named for the emperor, beautiful, blond and strong. But not strong enough.* Tears flooded her brilliant green eyes as she remembered the day she'd realized his will wouldn't last, that he was turning. It had taken every last ounce of her resolve to take him past the point of loss of soul, all the way to destruction, but she'd done it. *I killed him to save him.*

I thought this time would be different. Nephilim are stronger than men, since they're semi-divine. Lucien should have been able to withstand my needs, but he left me. In some ways, it was harder than Alexander's death, because with Lucien she'd dared hope. Her hunger grew, but she felt no desire to fill it. The gnawing her belly made her nauseous, but the thought of pursuing other food, of seeking out people coupling in dark corners and feeding on their passion, actually made it worse. She gagged at the thought.

After Lucien, no one will satisfy me again. I wonder if, in this present apathy, I could actually starve myself to death. The way I feel, it won't take long, and I honestly don't care.

She closed her eyes and willed sleep to come. The desert sun beat down on her milky skin. She couldn't burn, so what difference did the heat make? She inhaled the clean, hot scent of the desert; of exotic flowers and scrub and the endless, baking sun. And then a familiar scent wended its way through to her senses. Her eyes shot open.

A dark shape knelt above her, the sun shining on ebony skin gleaming with sweat. He'd shaved off his hair, but those burning dark eyes boring down into hers with no less intensity for the weeks that had passed.

"Lucien?"

"I'm here, my love." He ran one hand down her arm, creating enticing tingles in her skin.

"Where were you?" she demanded.

"I am still one of the Nephilim," he reminded her. "I have work to do."

"Killing my sisters."

He didn't try to deny it. "Yes."

"Why didn't you kill me, Lucien, when we met?" she demanded. "You should have."

"I couldn't, Sarahi. You're not like the others."

"How could you know that from such a brief conversation?"

His lips curved into a wistful smile. "I knew before you opened your mouth. It's your aura, love. It's so beautiful. No one evil would have such a lovely pink aura." He ran a hand inches from her face, as though touching her. Though his skin did not make contact with hers, she shivered. "Evil makes an aura black, but yours isn't even purple. It shines like the sunset. I could never kill such a beautiful soul."

A demon with a beautiful soul? How can that be true?

His lips met hers, submerging her self-doubt under a deluge of affection. They kissed for endless moments, at last satisfying Sarahi's appetite. She was full to overflowing long before he lifted her simple cotton sundress over her head, lowered her to the ground, and covered her with his body.

By the time his hands went to her breasts, lifting the heavy globes to taste and pleasure her aching nipples, the only hunger she felt was her own desire for her lover. She traced her fingers over the smoothness of his shaven skull, down the back of his neck, and between his powerful shoulder blades.

* * *

Lucien shivered as her skillful fingers tickled and aroused him. This time he wanted to take the lead. He'd spent more time than he should have over the last six weeks observing the men who were drawn to Succubi, wanting to learn what they knew so he could use it on his own beloved.

He trailed his lips down the center of her body, kissing her belly and then dipping lower. Sarahi moaned and parted her thighs, so he could move lower yet, kissing the scarlet curls. He parted them with his tongue, tasting the lush wetness of her intimate folds. He found the swollen center of her pleasure and worked it with delicate precision, bringing her to a hard, shrieking climax.

Sarahi clawed at the earth as her pleasure washed over her. Her whimpers of delight nearly shattered his will. *It's time for me to be inside her again.* He ran one last thorough lick over her heated flesh before working his way back up the midline of her body. He paused a moment over her belly, listening to some unknown sound before shrugging and moving on. At last, he covered her body. She twined her legs around his hips and urged him closer.

He needed no further instruction. *I know just where she wants, where I want to be.* He rocked forward, filling her completely. Her nails clawed his back as he thrust into her tight, clenching flesh. A second, wilder peak broke over her, and she wailed. The sound of her ecstatic cries carried on the desert wind as he pounded into her until his own climax took him.

Heart thundering, Lucien withdrew from Sarahi's body and rolled them onto their sides. He looked into the beautiful green eyes of his beloved. She sighed with satisfaction.

"Is everything all right, love?" he asked her.

"It is now," she replied, her voice slow and sinuous as she trailed her fingers over his heated flesh, "but next time you need to go away, love, please tell me. I didn't know where you were. I thought you had left me."

"I could never leave you," he vowed. *I learned that quickly enough.*

"Then all is well." She pressed her lips to his shoulder.

And yet... that strange sound... "Are you certain?"

"Why do you ask?"

He cupped her belly. "Something felt strange here."

She bit her lip. "Well, I have been unusually hungry," she admitted.

"Oh." He glanced away, trying not to think about how she must have satisfied her hunger in his absence.

"But I didn't feed. I couldn't. I only wanted you."

He looked at her, confused. "What does that mean?"

"I have no idea. I worried I might be losing control of myself, but that should take months."

"Lie back."

Sarahi rolled onto her back and Lucien pressed his ear to her belly. *This does not sound like hunger. It does not gurgle. It pulses.* His eyes narrowed. "Love, can Succubi conceive?"

He met her eyes again and saw hers widen. "Not that I'm aware of. Only Mother is strong enough for that."

"Mother?"

"Lilith," she admitted.

I have heard the legend that the Succubi are descendants of the demon queen. "Ah, yes. I recall. Sarahi, there is something alive inside you."

Her delicately arched brows drew together. "What?"

He laid a hand on the gentle curve of her belly. "If you were human, I would say you were with child."

She sat up, shaking her head. "No Succubus has ever conceived a child."

He swallowed hard. "Nonetheless, I believe that you have."

"It cannot be."

"Feel for yourself."

Sarahi closed her eyes and reached inward, considering. Then her jaw dropped. "Lucien!"

"I know." He gathered her tenderly into his arms and carried her inside the trailer.

Chapter 6

The Mojave Desert, 1979

It turned out a pregnant Succubus was not that different from a pregnant human. As Sarahi's belly expanded, her hunger grew exponentially, and like a human woman, only certain foods appealed to her. She was no longer able to take nourishment from any source other than the sweet love energy of her angel.

Lucien fed her lavishly, filling her greedy belly with the choicest of pleasures, spending so much time with his lady that he faced discipline more than once for not being where he was supposed to be. *It's my own fault. She is so luscious I can't stay away.*

He never told her she was draining him. The more energy he gave to the sustaining of their child, the weaker he became. *How could I say a word? She would be consumed with guilt, and for naught, because the baby needs to be fed, and this is the only nourishment its mother can take.*

Still, it was a relief, on that Midsummer's Eve, when Sarahi woke with a start, wracked by labor pains. Lucien summoned the Indian woman who had agreed to act as midwife, and the two of them oversaw the birth.

As the dawn pierced the horizon, Sarahi gave a long, loud wail and the midwife scooped into her arms a tiny, squalling bundle of limbs with a wisp of fuzzy dark hair.

Lucien kissed his lady, proud of her strength, while the midwife cleaned and examined the baby. Then she laid him tenderly in Sarahi's arms and showed the Succubus how to place her son on her breast.

Lucien looked on, pride swelling his heart. *I'm blessed beyond what my kind could ever have expected.* Sliding his arm around her pale shoulders, he kissed the fiery hair at her temple.

A boy...that's good. At least I don't have to try to be father to a Succubus. He's going to grow up to be a fine, strong Naphil. "What should we call him, love?"

"I think... Josiah," she replied.

"Josiah. Excellent. I like that." He leaned over and kissed the baby, too.

Chapter 7

Lucien had been gone for five weeks. The work had been excruciating, long and dangerous. Several of his fellow Nephilim had not returned, but Lucien had been determined to survive. He had others relying on him now.

In truth, this was the reason his kind vowed celibacy. The responsibility of caring for a woman and a child meant he was not able to throw his life away in pursuit of his mission. But the moment he'd tasted the sweetness of Sarahi's kiss that long-ago day in Rome, this conclusion had become inevitable. *I have no regrets.*

He found his lady inside the trailer, sitting on the bed, propped up on pillows, their son cuddled to her breast. As she fed the baby, tears spilled down her cheeks. Her slender shoulders shook with quiet sobs.

She's been so emotional all through the pregnancy and even more now that our son is here. Who would have guessed that what I thought was a demoness to be fought was really just a woman desperate to be cared for?

"What's wrong, my love?" He slid into the bed beside her, stroking the tawny skin of his son's cheek where it touched her pale flesh.

"Oh, Lucien!" She leaned against his shoulder and wept as though her heart were breaking.

He stroked the scarlet silk of her hair, waiting for the storm to pass, wondering what on earth had upset his lady so much. "Talk to me, Sarahi. What is it?"

"It's the baby," she wailed.

"What? Is he ill?" Lucien examined the healthy glow of his son's skin, the plump rolls of flesh around his thighs, belly and chin. *He's a little dumpling of a child.* Lucien couldn't help but smile at the boy, who looked so appealingly like a mixture of the two of them.

"No. Worse. You can't imagine how bad." Sarahi's obvious distress at last drew his attention back to her.

"Why?"

"Lucien, look at him."

Josiah had finished nursing, and she lifted him to his father, showing Lucien the brilliant green eyes shining from the dark face. Milk dribbled down the baby's dimpled chin.

Lucien stroked his son's fuzzy hair. "How nice, love. He has your eyes."

"Demon eyes," Sarahi insisted, sounding hysterical.

Lucien tried to soothe her. "So, he takes after you in some ways. He's a boy. Therefore, he's a Naphil."

"No, love. He's not." She wiped her cheeks with the back of one hand.

"There's no such thing as a male Succubus," Lucien pointed out.

She sobbed. "If only that were true. Haven't you heard the legend of the Incubus?"

"Bah." Lucien waved away Sarahi's claim. "Old wives' tales. There's never been such a creature."

"Lucien," Sarahi protested, "he takes my energy with the milk, I can feel it. He is an Incubus. This is terrible."

He shook his head, trying to understand both what Sarahi meant and what its implications could be. "Is that really such a bad thing? Legend says the Incubus will have incredible powers. With us to teach him right from wrong, he'll be an agent for good."

Sarahi shook her head. "Do you remember the day we met?" She struggled visibly to control herself as she spoke.

"Of course." *I wonder where she's headed with this.*

"I told you our kind fed because we had no choice?"

He looked at her but said nothing.

She closed her eyes. "It's true, but not the whole truth. We feed, and in the feeding, our men are weakened. Eventually, this weakening damages their souls and destroys their will. They become enslaved."

Her words struck like hammer blows on Lucien's heart. "Is this the fate you had in store for me?" he roared. "To be your captive angel?"

"No!" she cried, reaching out to him. He ducked back. Her dainty hand closed into a fist and fresh tears streamed down her cheeks. "Never that! I love you, Lucien. I believed you would be strong enough, and I would not be able to harm you in that way." She reached out again, and this time he allowed the touch. *I never knew love until I knew this woman. She wouldn't set out to harm me.* He forced himself to listen. "At any rate, those men are not enslaved to the Succubus. If I turned you, I would not be able to keep you. You would belong to our mother. To Lilith. Men are brought to her and become her property."

"To what end? Are they her army?"

Sarahi laughed, a little hysterically. "How like a warrior. No, love... well yes, they fight if necessary, but no. They are drones."

His dark eyebrows came together in consternation.

"Like bees, Lucien. She's the queen. Their job is..."

"To breed." He scowled.

Sarahi winced. "Yes. She is the only one of us with pure demon blood. Our half-demon heritage is not strong enough to take a man's seed. Only she can breed with them. That is how the Succubi are created."

"So, she really is your mother?" *I thought that was just a saying.*

"Yes." Sarahi inhaled deeply, causing her plump breasts to roll. Then she spoke again. "The Succubi are not truly her goal."

There's more? Good Lord! "Then what, Sarahi? What does she want? What are we fighting against?"

She broke eye contact, her gaze skating away. "She has been trying for centuries to have a son."

He looked at her profile in silence while the implications sank in. "She's trying to create an Incubus?" he asked at last.

"Yes. If it is her son, she will have control. She can finally have her revenge." The despair she felt twisted her face.

I still don't understand. "Love, your mother is a powerful demoness, nearly a goddess. Against whom does she seek revenge?"

Sarahi sighed, refusing to meet Lucien's eyes. "Against all the children of Adam, and the One who loves them. She has nurtured her hatred and humiliation for millennia. She believes with the power of the Incubus under her control, she can enslave all the children of Adam, thereby inflicting the ultimate suffering on..."

"The Creator." *I wish to Heaven I still felt confused.*

"Yes." She finally met his gaze, her expression stricken.

"But, Sarahi, this is not her son. He's ours," Lucien pointed out.

"Do you honestly think that will stop her?" Sarahi cried, growing wild again. "When she finds out he exists, she will claim him. It's only a matter of time. Just last week, one of my sisters came by to visit and asked why I was cradling a baby."

Lucien stared at his lady, horrified.

"I told her I was trying to seduce his father. She thought it was a great joke, but that story won't hold forever. *She* will eventually find out and take him from me. She'll turn him. Oh, Lucien, you should have killed me when you had the chance."

She sniffled. He gathered her into his arms, the baby cradled between their bodies. She hid her face against his shoulder.

"No, my love. I could never kill you. I love you." He stroked the burgundy silk of her hair.

She covered his hand with hers. "And I love you, Lucien. That is why I need your help."

"Anything, my love."

She rested her head on his shoulder, her whole body trembling. "You have to take the baby. Hide him. Hide him where even I cannot find him. Take him to a place where he will be safe." He could feel her burning tears rolling down his shoulder.

He tucked one finger under her chin and lifted her face. "Take Josiah? Love, how will you stand it?"

"You have to. I don't want him going to her. It's best this way." Her voice broke. She drew an unsteady breath and continued. "You have to go away from me too. I can't have you near me. If we created one Incubus together, we could create another."

The thought of losing his beloved tore deep into his heart. "I won't leave you, Sarahi."

"You must." She clutched his shirt in one fist. "You have to raise our son. Teach him what is right. Teach him to be good, to be light, so he won't be swayed by *her* temptation."

He looked down into her glimmering green eyes. *Lord, I hate it, but she's right. This must be done.* He lowered his lips to hers in the most heart-wrenching of kisses. "I will for now, my love, but we will be together again someday, I swear it. I love you, Sarahi."

"And I love you, Lucien."

She clutched the baby close to her breast, then lowered him a bit, looking down at his little face as love and despair warred in her expression. She touched her lips to his forehead. "I love you, my little one." Her voice broke. Tears splashed on the baby's nose and she kissed him again and again.

At last, she hesitantly extended Josiah. "Take him while I can still let him go!" she wailed.

Lucien gathered their son into his arms and stood, turning as though to leave. Then he glanced back. "Swear me a vow, my love."

"Anything."

"Don't starve. Live. Wait for me."

She nodded. He transported. The sound of Sarahi's heartbroken sobs rang out across the nighttime silence of the desert.

Part II

Chapter 8

A remote part of Central Montana, 1989

"Mr. Smith, tell me the story again," ten-year-old Josiah begged. "Tell me about my father."

"Joe, I've told you three times this week." The silver-haired black man sighed, frustrated by his young student's pestering.

"It's okay, Josiah," Annie replied. "I remember it. I'll tell you."

Josiah smiled, white teeth flashing in his café au lait face, in no way deterred. "I want to hear it from your grandpa," he told his friend.

"Well, Josiah," Mr. Smith replied, "I'll consider it... after practice."

Josiah commenced to whining as only a small boy can, but Mr. Smith put his hand on the child's thin back and ushered him out of the central meeting hall of the compound to the courtyard. Annie trailed along, trying not to look too eager. *Why doesn't Josiah like practice? I love it! I'd do it every day if I had the chance!*

But today, it seemed, Grandpa felt traditional. Maybe the sight the other elder clerics patrolling the shooting range had something to do with it. *Those old men and women don't care for the sight of a pistol or rifle in the hands of a young girl.*

Grandpa handed the semi-automatic handgun to Josiah. "Now remember, boy, aim only at the target."

Josiah sulked as he trained the weapon on the hastily-drawn silhouette of a woman that had been tacked to a hay bale.

"Imagine it's a Succubus. You don't want her to get a chance to come after you. Take her down."

The boy aimed, fired, and missed. The recoil nearly knocked Josiah on his butt.

Annie grinned. *I can control a pistol. It's easy for me. But I grew in the last year and Josiah is still little-kid small.* Annoyed at being left out of target practice, Annie crept away from her grandfather, who was showing Josiah—again—how to strengthen his stance to compensate for the recoil. She crossed to the far corner of the flat expanse of treeless grass that formed the courtyard. There, against a white stone wall, a small pavilion with a bright green roof and matching columns provided shade for the six ancient specimens who, along with Grandfather, provided leadership to the Order of Clerics.

She stood behind one support column and peeked at the group. *They're so OLD. That one there must be forty!* Unabashedly nosy, she eavesdropped on their conversation.

"Yes, I know he's a unique creature, but so far he shows signs of being nothing more than what he is... a weak Naphil. He's proven himself slower, smaller, and less adept than any of his brethren," said a woman with white hair like meringue, styled in a puffy bouffant on top of her head.

"He's young," retorted a balding gentleman with huge glasses like car windshields perched on a short, upturned nose. "And it's been millennia since there was a new Naphil. Maybe they develop more slowly."

"Ha!" laughed a third, another man, this one with a nimbus of silver hair and deep wrinkles on his cheeks. "He's only one-quarter angel, three-quarters human. We should train him as a cleric and forget about the rest. How's his father? Is he out of confinement yet? No one fights like Lucien."

"He is to be released later this week," said the first woman, resting her hand on one of the rough-hewn columns.

From across the lawn, the pistol sounded another deafening blast. Annie turned to look. This time Josiah actually sprawled on the ground. *The shot went wide again, I see.* The target tacked to the hay bale remained unblemished. Grandfather reached down and hauled the boy to his feet, quickly averting his face. Annie saw the flash of irritated amusement.

A sigh from behind her brought Annie's attention back to the elders.

"We'll be lucky if he even manages to become a decent cleric," said Nimbus.

The others nodded solemnly. Then Windshield Glasses added, "As many Nephilim as we've lost in just my lifetime, I had such high hopes."

"Stop, friends," said Bouffant. "We are not alone. Come out, little one. We know you're there."

Annie's stomach swooped. Face burning, she stepped out from behind the column.

"Eavesdropping, were you?" Bouffant asked her, scowling.

Annie gulped and nodded. No point in lying. She'd already been caught.

"Why?" Bouffant asked, her expression more unwelcoming than ever.

Instead of answering the question, Annie posed one of her own. "You were talking about Josiah, weren't you?"

"What concern is that of yours?" the elder snapped.

"He's my friend," she retorted, refusing to be cowed. "There's nothing wrong with him."

"Oh, child. If only that were true," Windshield Glasses stepped over to her and placed one heavy hand on her slender shoulder. "But don't worry. We'll train him up. He'll become a warrior yet. Believe it."

"Oh, I do," Annie replied, pushing a lock of bushy, light brown hair off her forehead and boldly meeting each set of eyes; blue, gray, and green, with her own dark brown ones. "He'll be the best of all of us. At least, as long as you refuse to let *me* train. After all, we have women senators and women ambassadors. Why not women warriors?"

"Now, now," Windshield Glasses patted her head soothingly. "When you get older, you'll understand. Battles are no place for a girl, and the one we're facing is so terrible. You'll be glad to hide away in the tower."

"Maybe *you* will," she retorted, jerking her head away from his hand, "but no matter what it takes, I'll be on the field with the warriors."

"Watch your tone," Bouffant snapped, but the two men laughed indulgently and shooed her away. Sulking, Annie crept back to target practice just in time to see Josiah fire another wild shot. This time he remained standing, but the bullet sailed high above the target, over the stone wall at the far side of the courtyard and embedded itself in a pine tree growing out of the hillside.

"Oh, for Heaven's sake," Annie sighed. She walked right up to Josiah and wrenched the gun from his hand, pushing him down with a nudge of her shoulder. "Do it like this." She aimed at the target and pulled the trigger, burying a bullet just to the left of the pseudo-Succubus's heart. "That's how you fire a kill shot," she told her friend. Then she tossed the pistol to the grass beside him and stalked back into the compound.

* * *

Three days later

Lucien stretched out to his full height. Not used to traveling by car, he'd been unprepared for the tight quarters. He had barely managed to squeeze his almost-seven-foot frame into the cramped interior, and then he'd been driven almost a full day without the chance to extend his limbs. *This is the last phase of my punishment.* During the long drive, he remembered the day it had begun.

He'd arrived at the compound ten years earlier. In this white block in the Montana wilderness, all clerics lived, and the Nephilim retreated to heal from injuries and rest after long campaigns. This time, he'd done the unthinkable. He'd arrived with an infant in his arms. The son of a Naphil. The day remained etched forever in his memory.

* * *

Bang! Bang! Bang!

"Stop that pounding, I'm coming," a cranky-sounding female voice responded to his knock. The door flew open to reveal Pearl Smith, a beautiful biracial girl who'd had a crush on Lucien when she was young. Two years married, she was expecting, and her belly swelled tremendously. *I think she must be about due to deliver.*

"Lucien!" she exclaimed, throwing her arms around him. He turned slightly to the side, protecting his precious bundle from her exuberance. "What do you have there?" she asked.

"I need to see your father," he replied, ignoring her question.

She frowned. "The elders are in a meeting..." she began, but Lucien cut her off.

"This is urgent. I must speak with him immediately. His heart pounded. *This is not going to go over well.*

Pearl nodded her light brown curls dancing with her movement. She seemed not to notice his discomfort. "Come on." She grabbed his arm and led him down a white-walled hallway to the conference room, where the elder clerics—all seven of them—sat around a wide oak table.

Surrounding them on all the walls, shelf after built-in wooden shelf groaned with books, all ancient, moldy, and warped. On the table lay a lambskin scroll. The margins of the document, as well as the spines of many of the books, bore a strange gilded image. A flared base tapered to a sharp point, like a fence finial. A gold circle was centered on the spike. Two blades, like back-curving daggers, crossed just below the circle, their handles affixed to the spike before crossing and curving down towards the base and upwards toward the point.

They tell me it's the symbol of the Incubus, though I've never much cared for prophecy, he thought. *Perhaps I should have paid closer attention.*

Heads of gray, white, silver, and one salt-and-pepper leaned over the treasured document. The shades had been closed to prevent sunlight from damaging the crumbling material, and only a small lamp illuminated the room. The darkness seemed to close in on Lucien like a physical touch. He longed for the hot, clean air of the desert, lightly perfumed with cactus flowers and Sarahi's sweet scent.

At the sound of the door bursting open, the four men and three women turned.

"Pearl," Mr. Smith exclaimed, "you can't just interrupt a meeting like that..."

"But, Father," the young woman insisted, not backing down from his disapproval, "Lucien has come. He needs to talk to you."

Fourteen eyes turned his direction. Their gazes felt like hot blades skewering into him. Embarrassment burned hot in his face.

"Well, Naphil, what is so very important you couldn't wait a few minutes to brief us?" the elder demanded.

"Mr. Smith, I..." He closed his eyes, unsure how to continue. *Be a man, Lucien. You fell in love. You created a child. For all other species, such things are a joy, worthy of a celebration. Only custom disallows this.*

"You what, Lucien?" the man said, rising and crossing to him, laying a hand on his arm. His eyes fell on the baby, and a smile carved grooves in the dark skin around his mouth. "And who is this little fellow? Just a few weeks old, I'll warrant. Goodness, he looks like Pearl did at that age. Whose baby is this, Lucien?"

"He's uh... mine," Lucien managed to force out at last.

Mr. Smith looked askance at him, his brown eyes huge with shock. Though nowhere near the age of the rest of the elders seated around the table, the force of his personality showed he would be in charge in due time. He had leadership stamped all over him. The surprised eyes crinkled at the corners and the full lips fell open in a loud laugh. "Yours? Lucien, you goof! I never knew Nephilim had a sense of humor."

"Um, we don't," he replied.

The laughter died instantly. Eight humans inhaled sharply.

"Lucien?" Pearl asked in a trembling voice.

Mr. Smith stared hard at the baby. Josiah yawned, his tiny mouth cracking wide. And then he opened his eyes and regarded the middle-aged gentleman with a puzzled expression.

Mr. Smith's eyebrows drew together. "He is yours. I can see that. So, Lucien, second in command of all Nephilim, a general in the army of half-angels, has broken his vows. Who, may I ask, is his mother?"

"That I will not say," Lucien replied. "But she did not abandon our child by choice. She's in a… dangerous situation." He looked down into the green eyes that so resembled his beloved's. *Now lost to me. This boy is all I have left.* His heart clenched, and his eyes burned. He looked up at the elder-in-training, his former sidekick, and let his desperation show. "I have broken my vow. I admit it. Punish me in any way you wish, but, please, help me care for my son."

Mr. Smith shook his head and opened his mouth to speak, but Pearl jumped in ahead of him.

"Of course, Lucien. Of course. He'll need to be fed. I think I can get one of the other mothers to feed him until…" She placed her hand on her belly. "And then I'll care for him myself. Nurse him myself. I promise you, no harm will come to your baby while I live." She leaned up. Lucien bent to receive the gentle touch of her lips on his cheek. He closed his eyes against a flood of relief, but a single tear escaped. With one arm holding Josiah, and the other around Pearl, no hand remained to wipe it away, and it slipped down the length of his cheek and dropped from his chin to the floor.

* * *

The car pulled to a stop and Lucien climbed out to stand before the same white stone wall he'd seen hundreds of times since the decision had been made to transfer one-fifth of the Nephilim to North America, in the year 1712.

This has been a center of angelic power long before even the distant cities of Billings, Helena, and Glendive were built, Lucien thought, reciting history in a vain attempt to keep his heart from pounding. *From there, it was easy enough to pop over to Virginia and keep an eye on the English settlers, to Louisiana to monitor the French, and to the southwest to watch the Spaniards for signs of demonic infiltration. Even now, we remain in relative isolation, despite the intrusiveness of the modern world. We Nephilim prefer it that way, as do the clerics, who support and fight alongside us. Without the clerics, the Nephilim could well have been wiped out by now.* It was to that body of human overseers Lucien had submitted himself for punishment.

Ten years had been his sentence. Ten years at a monastery in Santa Fe, among human monks, far from his work, his friends, and most painful of all, his son. A decade not knowing what had become of Sarahi. How it had gnawed at him, the fate of his beloved and his child being completely out of his hands. He had dedicated himself to the training prescribed for him, the deprivation and the silence. *At last, that time has passed. Someday I will find Sarahi, but now I need to see Josiah.*

As he followed the young cleric who had driven the car across a rugged gravel parking lot along a barely visible path over the hill and between dense pine trees to the hidden compound, he wondered if his boy had grown like a human or Naphil. At ten, a human child would be poised on the brink of adolescence. Half-angels matured much more slowly. Lucien had experienced puberty at the age of forty, just after the Great Flood.

"Lucien."

He blinked, shaken from the encroaching memories. The cleric opened a heavy wooden door and stood beside it, urging Lucien to enter.

"Thank you," he told the boy. "What is your name?"

"Tom," the youth replied, tossing a strand of shaggy brown hair out of his eyes.

Lucien nodded to Tom and entered the compound. The letter he'd received told him to meet the elder council in their conference room, so he proceeded directly there.

Inside, Lucien found Mr. Smith waiting for him in the familiar book-laden room, beside the oversized conference table. *Goodness, he's aged. I didn't expect the change to be so dramatic.* Even factoring in human life expectancies, it seemed more than a decade showed in Mr. Smith's face. Two children, a boy and a girl, stood beside the old man. Though the girl was taller, the two looked enough alike to be siblings. That is, until their faces turned up to him. One, with warm brown eyes and delicate features, resembled Mr. Smith. *This is probably the baby Pearl was carrying when I brought Josiah to the compound.* The other... Those piercing green eyes told him everything he needed to know.

"Josiah?"

"Father?" The little boy met his eyes and he returned the long gaze in silence, one that contained at once apology, grief, longing, and fear. Then the child, not restrained by millennia of training, broke composure and dashed across the room. Lucien caught him right up off his feet and squeezed him. *By all heaven, he smells like Sarahi.* Lucien's throat burned.

"Please, Father," the little boy begged. "Don't go away, again."

"No, son. I'm here. I'm here now."

Chapter 9

Sarahi crept into the chamber, trying to remain unobtrusive. *It's necessary every so often to appear before Mother to pay homage, leave offerings, but I hate it.* Each time she faced the demoness, it reminded her of her son, lost to her, perhaps forever, and of the Naphil she had loved. *If I had a choice, I would leave and never come back.* But she could not. The danger was too great. Too much depended on her behavior remaining above reproach.

At least it's an easy place to feed. She moved through the dim light of a black fire that crackled and flickered in the center of the room. It gave off no heat, leaving the chill of stone and the strange atmosphere of this otherworldly place to hang heavy in the chamber. She clutched her scarf to her head for warmth. *Modesty means nothing here.* She could feel her eyes glowing in the darkness. Like a cat, she could reflect even the faintest scrap of light. From the corners of the room, other lamp-like eyes glowed. Sarahi approached the altar and laid down her offering of flowers and fruit.

A familiar sound rang through the room, drawing her attention. She'd seen this spectacle thousands of times. As expected, a new drone was servicing the demon queen. *Another Succubus will soon be joining our ranks.* Sarahi smirked. She now knew no matter how many drones her sisters provided, no Incubus would ever be born here. Only the combination of Succubus and Naphil proved potent enough to create the coveted creature of legend.

Her heart clenched at the memory of her lover and their son, lost to her all these years. *To create a world where we can all be together, I would sacrifice everything.*

She looked towards the throne on its dais again. Lilith appeared to be a lovely creature. Her snowy skin possessed an internal luminescence. She glowed like light brought to life. Her eyes, solid green and completely lacking in pupils, shone with pleasure. She sprawled, one leg dropped over each heavily carved arm of her wooden throne. Spread wide, the towering demoness accepted the enthusiastic possession of a young, blond man with a muscular physique. His back was to the room as he copulated with the demon queen, his buttocks thrusting obscenely.

Ironically, though this young man was essentially dead, his lust remained potent. Sarahi's hunger eased instantly. *It's a rotten way to feed, but an effective one.*

The young man groaned in completion and Lilith shoved him away with her bare foot. He stumbled, regained his footing, and stood naked beside her, his genitals gleaming in the aftermath of the encounter.

The demoness stretched luxuriously and lowered her legs to the floor. Sitting up tall, her naked body glowed in the darkness. To many, she would appear beautiful, especially nude like this. Her scarlet nipples gleamed like rubies, her eyes reflected the light of the fire to shine like emerald lamps. *I do not see her as beautiful, I see only the insatiable lust for power. To have so much and appreciate so little... I would have been content to live out my endless existence in a travel trailer at the edge of the desert with my lover and my son. That was a blessed life for the short time I had it. I want it back.*

"Sarahi." The deep, cold, resonant voice carried through the room. *Mother recovers quickly from her exertions.*

"Mother." her own voice had been carefully cultivated over centuries of experience into the perfect degree of groveling submission.

"Come here, my little one."

She approached the throne nervously.

"Take off that foolish scarf."

Sarahi dropped her shawl around her shoulders, letting her scarlet hair spill free. She suddenly felt more naked than the unclad demonesses surrounding her.

Lilith rose from her throne, towering over her tiny daughter and staring down at her with displeased eyes. Sarahi bowed her head.

"Why is it, my dear, that you never bring me any drones? All your sisters have done it. All but you. Why?"

It's a good thing I anticipated the question, or I'd have had no idea what to say. She willed herself to look ashamed and said, "I am sorry, Mother. I can never get a man to stay with me long enough."

"What a pathetic Succubus you are, Sarahi. I can't imagine how you came from me. Bringing you into the world was a waste of my time." Lilith sighed in deep disgust and beckoned. "Come closer. I have a task for you."

Sarahi suppressed a sigh of her own and stepped up to the dais. Lilith's long, black-taloned hand shot out, catching her around the throat. The claws dug into her flesh.

"You must try harder, little one. If you do not provide me with what I need, you're no further use to me, and I might just decide to devour you. Do you understand?" Oddly for such dark words, her tone remained light, as though threatening her daughter with cannibalistic destruction were no great matter.

"Yes, Mother," Sarahi replied, her voice as neutral as she could make it around the crushing pressure.

The claws loosened. The little Succubus made no move to step back. She had not been invited to do so. Instead, she waited, apparently at perfect peace with whatever end her mother had planned for her.

Lilith turned towards her drone. "Come," she said. He approached. "Sarahi, fetch my cup."

Sarahi hurried to obey the command, her stomach clenching in disgust over what she knew was coming. *I wish there was some way to prevent this, but there's nothing I can do. Sadly, what is at stake is more important than this one life.*

The demon queen rose approached her meal. His nearly six feet of height appeared insignificant against her towering stature. She grasped his shoulders in her clawed hands and lifted him.

For a moment his blue eyes filled with awareness. As Sarahi watched in horror, his pleading gaze shot to her. She could see his fear. And then the demoness opened her mouth. Long, inward-curving fangs extended from her gums and she sank them deep into his unguarded throat. She yanked her head back, tearing out an obscene hunk of flesh. Blood sprayed, rolling down her breasts in a scarlet river. Everywhere the blood touched her, it glowed in the light of her luminescence. She chewed the mouthful and swallowed it, licking blood from her lips with relish, and then nodded to her daughter. Sarahi extended the golden chalice beneath the twitching corpse of her mother's latest victim and caught the spilling tide as best she could. It sprayed across her face, running down like the tears she didn't dare to shed.

For today, at least, I'm safe.

Chapter 10

"Father," Josiah said softly, entering the dormitory where Nephilim stayed when they were at the compound. The soft colors of the bedspread on which Lucien sat—red fading through the shades of orange and rose to gold—seemed to mean something to the half-angel. His obsidian eyes remained fixed on the windowpane as he ran his fingers over a band of delicate shell pink. Perhaps he, like his son, felt the Montana winter leeched all the color out of the world. Beyond the small, high window, snow swirled in a chill wind that could be felt even through the cinderblock walls of the compound.

"Josiah?" Lucien's expression returned to the present, to his thirteen-year-old son standing in front of him.

"Father, you don't have to live here, do you?" Josiah asked. "Can't you live anywhere and just stop in here to get orders and be debriefed and stuff?"

"That's right, son. Why do you ask?" Lucien patted the bed beside him, but Josiah felt too squirmy to sit.

"Well..." The boy stared down at the toe of his sneaker. *While the other boys my age are outgrowing clothes and shoes faster than any of the ladies could keep up with, I've been the same size since I was ten. Tiny. Annie towers over me now, close to adult height.*

"Well what, son? What's wrong?" Lucien rose from his seat on the edge of the bed and placed his hand on Josiah's shoulder. The boy looked up the huge line of his father's frame to his face. *I wonder if I'll ever be tall like an average human, let alone like a Naphil.* "I don't want to live here anymore. I don't like this place. Mr. Smith has never liked me, and he's in charge of all the trainees. He thinks I'm useless."

"You're not useless, son," Lucien said kindly.

"Are you sure, Father?" Josiah shot back. "I'm small. I don't think I'll ever grow. I'm too small to handle the smallest gun. I can't even lift a broadsword. The only weapon I'm good with is a throwing star. What's the point of that?"

Lucien's dark brows drew together. "And so? Who said you needed to grow like a human? I'm not surprised you're taking your time. In fact, I'd be shocked if you grew at a human pace. You're part angel. We develop more slowly. I was child-sized until I was nearly forty."

Josiah blinked, startled by the information. "Why don't the elders know that?"

Lucien smiled, but it always looked sad. *Why are you so sad, Father? What would give you a reason to smile for real?* "I'll explain it to them," Lucien promised. "Be patient, son. They're fully human. Though we call them 'elders', they live human life spans. The last Naphil was born around the time of the Great Flood. No one alive remembers us as children."

"I see, sir." Josiah met his father's eyes and saw the warrior react, as he always did. A wave of grief like a tsunami rolled over the chiseled face. *It just kills me that something about me makes Father so sad. Aren't fathers supposed to be proud of their sons? To be happy about them? Yes, he was punished, but that ended three years ago. Shouldn't he be over it by now?*

Pretending his face didn't look like the weight of the world rested on him, Lucian replied lightly, "Rest easy. You are normal, as far as I can tell. I will let them know you might need extra time to grow up, because of your unusual nature."

Josiah nodded. "Thanks, Father, but I still don't like it here. Apart from Annie, no one really cares for me. They think I'm strange. I wish I could go somewhere else, somewhere with people who don't know there are half-angels, who will think I'm just a kid and treat me like I'm normal."

Lucien chuckled without humor. "From what I've seen, no thirteen-year-old gets to feel that way. They all struggle to fit in, not realizing it's impossible. I think you'll just need to ride out these transitional years. Hold on, son. There's life on the other side."

"Yes, but, Father, what will I be when I'm done?" Josiah demanded. "I keep hearing things like 'weak Naphil'. Is that what I am?"

Lucien paused, weighing his words. "I wish I could answer that. I don't know, and I won't until you gain more maturity, what traits you have inherited from me, from humanity, and from your mother."

Mother. He actually mentioned her. Josiah leaped on the opportunity. "Father, what was Mother like? Who was she?"

The obsidian eyes went hazy with thought again. "Your mother was... is... the most beautiful, brave, amazing creature who ever existed, apart from you. She..." He trailed off, shaking his head. "There are no words. She had... the most beautiful soul, the most shining pink aura. It was clean, like the sky at dawn. I was blessed to know her."

"If she's so perfect," Josiah said, hearing the hard bitterness in his own voice, "then why did she give me away? Is there something so wrong with me that my own mother doesn't want me?"

Black fire flashed in his father's eyes and Josiah took a step back. "Never say that again. It killed her to part with you. She loved you so much, she didn't dare expose you to the danger she lives in every day. She sent you away to protect you, and that is why you're here. Being what you are, there is no better place. I will not nullify her sacrifice by putting you in danger. Not for adolescent angst. You're staying. Go back to your training."

Stung, Josiah sulked out of the room. *Father won't listen to me. No one will. It's so unfair.*

* * *

That night, Josiah had his favorite dream. In it, his underdeveloped, childlike body was drawn into a warm embrace on a soft lap. A haunting fragrance enveloped him.

"Josiah," a quiet voice murmured in his ear, "I love you, my son."

In the dream, he knew who addressed him, and responded without reservation. "I love you too, Mother. I miss you. Where are you?"

"I am always with you, my love. I will never leave you. Darling Josiah. Be brave. Learn all you can. I will come to you when I am able. But no matter what, I have always loved you."

The hazy image resolved into the shape of a woman. Instead of the peach skin and red hair he knew she should have, she was entirely pink, like a sparkling rose-colored gem, though she felt soft where she touched him. She stroked his face and pressed a gentle, tingling kiss to his forehead.

"I miss you, Mother," he whispered. "Do you have to leave?"

"Not yet," she replied. "Let me hold you a little longer. You're getting so big."

He smiled.

* * *

The good mood Josiah's favorite dream brought only lasted until mid-morning. At first, practice had gone well. He'd been working out and running, and he finally had gained enough strength to fire some of the guns without being knocked over by the recoil. For the first time, he'd actually managed to hold the shotgun steady enough to hit the corner of the target, a feat he equated with winning a marathon. Goodness knew it had taken him long enough to get there.

"Well done!" Annie said, hugging him around the shoulders. "Try again."

Josiah lifted the shotgun to his shoulder. This time, Annie stood behind him, lending the strength of her almost adult-sized body to his. Though thirteen, he still looked no more than ten. The others boys' voices were breaking, and they were comparing the fuzz that had begun to appear on their chins and under their arms. *My skin is still smooth, my voice a pure alto. Will I ever grow up?*

But in one way he was maturing. The warmth of Annie's arms around him, the sweet girl-scent of perfume and shampoo, caused reactions he blushed to describe but felt nonetheless.

Trying to dispel images he knew would get him hit, if he dared hint at them aloud, he concentrated on the target and fired. With Annie's support, the shot fanned out from a perfect spot just to the left of the bulls-eye.

"Wonderful!" she exclaimed, squeezing his waist and leaning around him to press a kiss on his cheek. His skin burned at the moist touch. *Someday, if I ever manage to grow up, I know exactly which girl I want to marry.* Quick as thought, he dropped the empty shotgun in the grass and turned. He wrapped his arms around Annie's neck and tugged her down, kissing her lips before she could wriggle away.

"Josiah!" she half-laughed, half-protested.

"I'm not sorry," he told her, his childish voice intense. "Someday, Annie, you'll be mine."

She laughed out loud this time. "You have some growing to do first, Joe."

"I know," he replied, "but when I do, be ready. Promise me, Annie. Promise you'll wait for me."

She considered him, and then nodded. "Okay, Josiah. I'll wait."

He beamed. His grin turned to a scowl as Peter, two years his senior and almost twice his size, strode across the courtyard and wrapped an arm around Annie's neck.

"Get off me," she hissed, elbowing him in the ribs.

"What? I saw you kissing this little shrimp. Wouldn't you rather have a real man?"

Annie's laugh this time dripped scorn. "You? A real man? Ha. I'd take Josiah over ten of you."

Peter took instant offense. Of course he did. "Freak," he told her, releasing her with a little shove that sent her sprawling on the grass. "What about it, shrimp? You man enough to fight for your girl?"

Josiah considered his opponent. *It would be great to knock this big bully on his ass, but I'm not certain I can manage it.*

"Remember what I told you."

Did Annie say that? He shook his head. *She didn't. Peter isn't looking at her, but I heard her voice clearly in my mind.* What had she told him? *'Don't fuss about your size. Use it to your advantage.' Then she taught me all kinds of girly fighting tricks.*

Josiah looked at Peter again. *I could take him down using Annie's techniques, but while I might win the battle, I would lose the war. This fight is man-to-man, and I have to fight like a man.*

Josiah narrowed his eyes and charged. Peter sidestepped him and stuck a foot out.

The ground rose up to meet Josiah with nauseating speed. He landed with a crunch that reverberated through his whole body.

What happened? One minute I was running, and the next... He stared at a line of ants making their slow way through the grass as he gasped for breath. The sound of loud brays of laughter rang in his pounding ears. Then a female voice shrieking unintelligible words. Josiah caught his breath and tried to use his arms to push himself to a sitting position. Agony wracked him, and he screamed.

"Josiah?" Annie's sweet voice sounded in his ear. "What's wrong?"

He couldn't answer, could only moan. Then he screamed again as she rolled him to his side.

"You asshole!" she hollered. "Look what you did! His arm is broken!"

Josiah got a hazy image of Peter shrugging nonchalantly. "He fell on it. He broke his own arm."

"You tripped him!"

"He charged. If he hasn't learned to fight better than that by now, there's no hope for him." The bully strolled away.

As Peter's bulky frame withdrew from Josiah's field of vision, he saw a crowd of women headed in his direction, Pearl – Annie's mother and head nurse – in the lead. *She'll fix me.* Josiah waved his good hand in front of his face, trying to dispel a cloud of black gnats that seemed to have come out of nowhere. He could hear them buzzing.

"Josiah, why didn't you use your techniques?" Annie demanded.

"Had to be man-to-man," he choked.

"Fool. Bullies don't fight like men." She sucked in a noisy breath that sounded like a sob.

"I'm better than he is," Josiah insisted over the pain that radiated to his shoulder.

"Maybe so, but you're still a fool."

He wanted to say more – to argue with her, to ask how she'd managed to speak inside his head, but the gnats crowded closer until they became flies, and then bees. Their buzzing drowned out his words and total blackness fell.

* * *

In some ways, Annie mused to herself, *the six weeks Josiah spent in a cast were good for him.* Being forced to use his non-dominant hand had strengthened him overall. His handwriting was worse than ever, but his aim with a handgun had improved, as had his accuracy with throwing stars. Once the cast came off, he'd have to retrain his left hand. She grinned. *Left-handed in Latin is sinistra. If only Josiah could act sinister, his size would be less of a detriment. Alas, he's open-hearted and sensitive. That makes him a great friend—maybe even a boyfriend someday, if he'd ever grow—but as the warrior all young men wanted to be, he comes up short.*

"Hannah, are you listening?"

Sorry, Grandfather," Annie said, her cheeks tingling with heat. "But please call me Annie."

"I did. Three times. Are you finally paying attention?" Moses regarded her with bushy black eyebrows raised.

"Yes, Grandfather," she replied, making a show of meekness.

"Good. Tell me the origin of the Nephilim."

Annie opened the Bible on her desk and turned to Genesis. She found the passage and began to read.

Chapter 11

"Medic! Medic!" Mr. Smith raced into the compound, clutching a bundle of limp, dangling limbs close to his chest. One foot hung at a strange angle and little drops of blood sprinkled the hallway floor behind him.

Lucien, who had been meandering past the front door, nearly got bowled over by the rushing cleric. He jumped out of the way.

"Smith, what happened?" he shouted. Then his mind pieced together what he was seeing. Frizzy brown hair. Long denim skirt. "What happened to Annie?"

Mr. Smith didn't even slow down. Lucien trailed him to the clinic. Smith set the girl gently on the bed.

Lucien was no medic, but he could see the girl had been through something terrible. *Her right ankle is clearly broken.* Blood flowed freely from a deep gash across her belly, another at her hairline.

"What happened?" he asked again.

"Medic! Nurse! Someone, come on!" Smith seemed on the verge of hysteria.

At the sound of the shouting, two women and a man rushed into the room. They took in the sight of the battered girl, whose blood stained the white sheets redder with every passing moment.

"What happened?" the medic asked, hurrying to the sink embedded in the exterior wall of the white cinderblock room. Beside him, the nurses pulled on gloves and scooped up cloths. One raced to Annie and pressed down on the abdominal laceration. "It's not that deep," she murmured.

"Smith, why is Annie here? Isn't she supposed to be out of town with her parents?" Lucien demanded, trying again to capture the elder cleric's attention.

At last, Smith answered. "She was. I don't know what happened. One minute I was in my study, and the next, that boy appeared, holding her. I have no idea what went on."

Lucien's head shot up and his eyes widened. *Josiah.* He'd been on vacation with Annie and her parents in Virginia. *How on earth did they suddenly appear here? Josiah doesn't know how to relocate, does he? Is he even capable of it? And if he appeared out of nowhere clutching a wounded and bleeding Annie, something terrible must have happened!*

Lucien didn't waste time running through the compound. He simply relocated to Smith's study.

At first, the room appeared empty. No one sat in the leather recliner by the window or the blue rolling chair at the scarred mahogany desk. He was about to leave when a small sound captured his attention.

He followed the quiet sob to the corner, where his fourteen-year-old son huddled, arms around his knees, tears streaming down his face. Josiah wasn't just crying, he could barely breathe with the force of his sobs as he slowly rocked back and forth.

"Son?"

The boy looked up, revealing blood smeared on his face. "Father!" He leaped from his curled-up position and threw himself against Lucien's chest.

Lucien embraced him. "What happened, son? Are you hurt? What happened to Annie?"

"They came. In the night. Don't know why. Killed... oh God... killed them all."

Lucien's alarm grew. He grasped Josiah's arms in his hands and gently set him back a bit, looking into his eyes. "Who was killed?"

"Everyone! Annie's mom and dad, her brother Jake. The Succubi... they came."

A sensation of dread flared in the pit of Lucien's stomach. "Did they hurt you?"

Josiah shook his head. "We..." he gasped. Sobbed again. "We were outside. Annie and I. We were looking at con... con... at the stars. Heard a sound... ran inside... there were four of them. They were...

oh God. Their claws... they were laughing... 'One less cleric and his spawn,' they said.... I was frozen..." He broke into more shattered sobs. This time it took several minutes for him to calm down enough to speak. "Annie rushed them, and they cut her up. Knocked her down. They... I... I don't know what happened then. I just... I just ran after her. Pushed one away. Grabbed her. I heard one say, 'demon eyes!' Then I was here."

"Oh no!" Lucien hugged his son tight again.

"Is Annie okay?"

"Yes, son. She's okay. The belly wound isn't that bad, and the others are fixable. You saved her, Josiah."

Josiah, it was clear, had no interest in being congratulated. He let go of his attempts to speak and just dissolved into hysterics. *And rightly so. He just saw a whole family murdered. And now we have a worse problem. Those Succubi know there is a boy with demon eyes somewhere in the world. Josiah will not be a secret for much longer.*

* * *

Clash! Clang! Scrape! The sound of sword-on-sword rang through the courtyard. Josiah met Peter's thrust with his sword. Turning rapidly, he slid his blade out from underneath before the brute strength of his eighteen-year-old opponent could crush him down. It had taken years, but Josiah had finally accepted that he had to use stealth and dexterity against Peter. Though at sixteen, he had finally grown and was experiencing puberty, he remained small for his age, much slighter than the other boys. But once he made peace with his size, he'd found ways to use it to his advantage. At least he'd finally caught up with Annie, who apparently had stopped growing. As Josiah whirled to avoid another slash with the blunted practice sword, he caught sight of her standing by the wall, watching.

She's grown beautiful in the last three years. So beautiful it hurts to look at her. Her light brown hair bounced in a halo of curls around her shoulders. Her brown eyes sparkled in the light, as did her straight white teeth. Seeing her, Josiah wanted to show off. He wanted to meet Peter's attack head-on and drive the bully away, but he knew from experience that the moment this kind of thinking took over, he would be finished.

Resisting the urge to rush his opponent, Josiah feinted, and when Peter reacted, he made a lightning-swift movement, changing his direction and hitting the bigger boy on the ribs with bruising force.

Peter cursed and swung wildly, which opened him to a hit on the shoulder. Josiah dropped his practice sword between his opponent's legs. A deft twist and Peter lay sprawled on the ground before him.

The bigger boy laughed. "You've learned some new tricks, shrimp. Not bad, but you'll never be a real man. By the time you reach adult size, it will be too late."

Knowing better than to rise to the bait, Josiah stretched out his hand. The rules of etiquette had been drilled into all the children, and he followed them without thought.

In a move that seemed faster than possible for such a bulky boy, Peter reversed their positions, throwing Josiah to the ground and placing a size fifteen sneaker on his throat. He pressed down just a little, enough to restrict Josiah's airway slightly.

"Too trusting," Peter sneered. "Too bad for you, shrimp. By the time you grow up, I'll have your pretty Annie all to myself. Just imagine it, you little worm. You'll be celebrating your twentieth birthday and I'll be screwing your girl." Peter laughed. He let just a hint more weight press down on Josiah's throat.

And then, without warning, Peter went flying across the courtyard, landing in a heap by the wall.

"I have something to say about that, you disgusting toad," Annie snarled. "Josiah, are you all right?" She knelt beside him.

Josiah blinked, wondering what had happened. It slowly dawned on him that Annie must have knocked Peter away from him. He ground his teeth. *Even a girl is tougher and stronger than me.* "I'm fine," he snarled, twitching her hand off his shoulder. "I don't need any help."

He hauled himself to his feet and stalked away, back towards the compound. *I've had enough practice for one day.*

* * *

"Father?"

Lucien looked up from the report he was writing.

"Do you have a minute?" Josiah stepped into the council chamber, massaging his throat. His voice sounded hoarse.

"Of course, son," Lucien replied, indicating the chair next to him. "What's on your mind?"

Josiah sat, nervously rubbing his hands over his dirty jeans. He then brushed his fingers through his hair anxiously, composing his thoughts. "I… I think I'm in love."

Lucien nodded. "Annie is a very special girl. I'm not surprised."

Josiah blushed but didn't deny it. "Do you think we'll ever be… together?"

Lucien considered for a moment. "I don't see why not."

"Mr. Smith hates me," Josiah said darkly.

Lucien smiled. *Teens are so dramatic.* "I don't think he does. Most likely he's concerned for his granddaughter is all. She's his last living relative. After he lost his wife to cancer all those years ago, and then Pearl and her husband, and Annie's younger brother in that Succubus attack, well it's not surprising he's protective of Annie."

"It's more than that, Father. He really does hate me. I can feel it," Josiah insisted.

"Son, I've known him for so long. Long before he was called mister by anyone. Back when he was Moses Smith, minor cleric. He was my sidekick, you know."

Josiah raised one dark eyebrow. "But he's so old."

"Don't forget, son, he's human. He has a human lifespan. He may seem old now, but I can clearly remember when he was born. He fought by my side in his twenties and thirties."

"How old are you, Father?" Josiah asked hesitantly.

"I don't exactly know," he replied. "It's hard to measure in human years. I was a young Naphil when the Flood occurred."

Josiah's eyes widened. "Do you remember it? What was it like? Did you lose many friends?" he babbled in a rush.

"Slow down, Josiah," Lucien said, laughing. "No, I didn't lose any friends. The people who lived back then were... horrible. Every bit as bad as the Scriptures say. They make some of the Succubi look like little lambs. Believe me, son, the Creator was right to wipe them out."

"But what was the Flood like? Can't Nephilim drown?"

"Of course, we can, and to be honest... I don't know how we survived it." He saw his son was about to interrupt with a barrage of questions and held up his hand. "The Flood was not meant for us; we were told that in advance. We protected Noah and his family, we brought the animals, and then, when the first drops of rain began to fall, we all went to sleep. When we woke up, the world had completely changed. So, I have no idea what happened to us in between, but it was obviously divine protection."

Josiah's mouth hung open. *Clearly, this information is more than he can comprehend. Truthfully, neither can I.*

"But, Father, how did the Succubi survive? They were alive then, right?"

"Yes, son, they were. There weren't as many. Lilith has been breeding for thousands of years since then. As for how they survived, I'm not sure of that either, except... I've always had the theory that the hive is not exactly on earth. And before you ask, I don't know where it is either. If we knew, we would have assaulted it centuries ago, before the numbers of Succubi and drones grew so great, but we've never been able to find them."

Josiah nodded. "Doesn't it bother you, all the things you don't know?"

"Sometimes," Lucien replied, "but I trust in the divine plan. The Creator has never led us astray. Even our mistakes can be used for good. Never doubt that, Josiah. No matter what happens, the Creator's plan has not faltered. It twists and turns along the paths we take, and still comes out just the way He intended. Have faith, son."

"If I could be with Annie, I would never doubt again. Can you even imagine, Father, what it's like to be so very in love?"

A wave of sorrow washed over Lucien. "I don't have to imagine, Josiah. I know."

"You do?" The teen regarded him with wide green eyes that seemed to burn into the depths of his soul.

"Of course," Lucien snapped a little more forcefully than he intended. Softening his tone, he continued, "Where do you think you came from? I would never have broken my vows for lust or curiosity. I loved your mother. I love her still."

"Then where is she?" Josiah asked bitterly. "Why has she never come to me? Did she not love you back? Or was it me she didn't want?"

"Stop that, Josiah," Lucien growled, his grief making his tone gruff again. "She loved me, and she loved you too. She would never have chosen to leave you."

"But she did leave," Josiah pressed. Lucien clenched his teeth. *Child, mercy, please.* But of course, his son offered no such reprieve. "Did she die?"

"I hope not." Shaking off thoughts of Sarahi, the half-angel turned the conversation to Josiah, hoping to connect with the youth. "Listen, what would you do for Annie, if she asked it of you? What would you deny her?"

"Nothing," Josiah said firmly.

"Really?" *Please try to understand, son.* "And what if she asked you to leave her? What if she asked you to take your baby and walk away? What if it was the only way to ensure the little one would grow up safe? Would you do it, Josiah? I know you didn't understand as a child, but you're nearly an adult. Can you imagine a love that great? A sacrifice that deep?" An image of her beautiful, haunted green eyes seemed to float before him. "She didn't give you up because of a lack of love, but because of an excess. She loved you too much to let you live in danger. And she's always in danger, son. The only way I can protect her is to stay far away..." Lucien's voice stopped. It didn't break, it just refused to come out, as though his throat had closed. He looked into his son's eyes again and saw Sarahi in those glowing depths.

His throat opened, and a flood of words spilled out. "If only I could express to you, son. Your mother was so... beautiful. So perfect. She was so very happy when she was pregnant with you, stroking her belly and singing. Her soul shone like a gemstone; pure, pink light. I loved just looking at her. Knowing it was my child growing inside her... sometimes I thought I would burst. Believe me, Josiah. You are loved and wanted."

His son swallowed hard but said nothing. At last, he nodded slowly, his expression considering. He reached out his hand and Lucien stood, hauling him into a tight hug. Then the boy trailed out, leaving his father alone with his memories and grief.

* * *

BANG. The bullet whizzed over the top of the target, over the wall, and thudded into the badly scarred trunk of a gnarled jack pine. Peter snarled in frustration. He glanced at Mr. Smith, who was regarding him with a questioning expression.

"What?" Peter asked, irritated beyond measure by that quizzical look.

"You're normally a crack shot, my boy. What's wrong with you today? That's the fifth one you've missed."

"I had a rough night," Peter answered, not really wanting to explain why he was in such a funk.

Mr. Smith didn't speak, just kept on giving him that annoying stare.

"Okay, I had a bad dream," he spat out at last.

"About what?"

Peter felt his cheeks burn. *The nightmare was such a stupid one.* "I'd rather not get into it."

"Dreams are important," Mr. Smith replied. "You might be a seer. Don't be embarrassed, just tell me."

Peter sulked but Smith did not relent.

"Fine," the boy burst out. "I dreamed I was lying on the ground. I was trapped and couldn't move. And... someone... Josiah was standing over me. He said, 'How do you like it, jackass?' and then he sort of... waved his hand, like he was picking something up. And then I woke up feeling like shit."

Smith scowled at the obscenity but said nothing.

"Stupid dream, right?"

Still, Smith didn't speak.

"It was just a dream, right?"

"I don't know. I've often wondered... after a confrontation with Josiah, more than one person has reported feeling... tired, drained. I don't know what it means. Maybe the boy is some kind of psychic vampire. I would give a lot to know who his mother was."

Peter scoffed. "What a lot of hooey," he sneered. "Psychic vampire?" He burst out laughing. *Smith's really on a roll today.*

"You'd be wise not to think yourself so clever," Smith told Peter, effectively shutting down his mockery. "There's a great deal in this world you don't understand."

Chapter 12

Montana 1998

"Come on, Josiah," Annie urged, lacing her fingers through her boyfriend's and running down the white-tiled floors of the compound. Class had just ended for the day, and the two trainees hurried outside to enjoy the late-spring freshness.

They passed by door after door of meeting rooms, classrooms, and apartment suites lining the hallways of their home, and out onto the soft spring grass. The breeze they generated with their movements smelled pine and flowers. Though a high, white-stone wall completely encircled the courtyard, the adept nineteen-year-olds scrambled over it, eager to escape into the hills beyond. First Josiah clambered to the top, tearing the knee out of his blue jeans on the rough stone, so a hint of café au lait-colored skin peeked through.

Bracing himself on the wall, he lowered his hand and grasped Annie's. She remained his match physically; tall, long-limbed, and strong. Despite the ankle-length skirt that hampered her movements, she managed to climb up. For a moment they stood side by side on top of the wall, surveying the wide-open land beyond the compound. Up to this point, the L-shaped structure had been their entire world. But now, facing adulthood, she felt curious—and knew Josiah agreed with her—about what might lay beyond the walls. *Apart from the uneven Montana landscape, that is.* From here, all they could see directly in front of them was a tree-covered hill. To the left, a deep depression in the earth had filled with soft grass and plants, creating a lovely meadow. To the right, level land stretched as far as the eye could see. Now, in May, fragrant wildflowers of astonishing colors covered every surface. Josiah hopped from the wall and helped Annie down, her long skirt billowing. He kissed her lips gently, and then they ran down the hill towards the meadow.

The warm spring sun beat down on them as they embraced in the hip-deep grass. *We've been doing this more and more lately. I'm starting to feel a little nervous about where it's all headed. Of course, I have every intention of marrying Josiah someday soon, but I'm quite determined to earn a white wedding. We seem to be rushing the fence a bit too fast.* The clerics promoted chastity but didn't always succeed. *I'm quite sure I've seen a little baby bump or two under the plain white wedding robes, but I don't want that. I want to wait. I'm not certain, however, what Josiah had in mind. He seems to want to get me alone so often. It's about time we talk about it.* "Josiah..."

Instead of listening, he cupped her face in his hands and kissed her. *Well, there's no harm in a kiss, right? We're practically engaged.*

She returned his kiss, snaking her long, slender arms around his neck and opening her mouth to his. *He's so sexy.* His full lips compressed hers as he tasted her deeply. She knew he'd never kissed anyone else; they'd shared their first embrace years ago, when he officially asked her to be his girlfriend. Despite his lack of experience, he'd needed no education whatsoever, as their first kiss had been just as intoxicating as this one. *It almost seems like he was born knowing how to please a woman. If so, being his wife will be... very nice. I can't wait.* The rules stated they couldn't marry before the age of twenty, but that was less than a year away. *No reason to put it off anymore. Enough kissing. We need to have this conversation.*

"Josiah..." she said, trying to begin the discussion, but his hand closed over her breast and her thought processes stopped completely. She experienced a brief sensation of falling while his arms around her back kept safe, and then she lay cradled by the earth, the tall grass waving around her head as her beloved lowered his mouth back to hers.

"I love you," she breathed. "I can't wait until we get married."

"I can't wait either," he said.

That doesn't mean the same things as what I said, the last part rational of her mind told her, but the thought floated away when he skimmed her white blouse upward, leaning over to press his full, sensuous lips against the flat plane of her belly. She laced her fingers into his coarse black hair. He nudged the shirt up with his chin and kissed her rib cage, kiss after burning kiss, nipping her skin. Annie whimpered.

"Josiah," she managed to force out while his mouth was otherwise occupied. "When do you want to get married?"

"I don't know," he muttered. He grasped her blouse in his teeth and lifted it higher, baring her breasts in the sunshine. She rarely bothered with a bra, small as she was, and Josiah took shameless advantage of that fact, lowering his mouth to one erect brown nipple and sucking it to a throbbing peak.

Annie moaned, her reticence floating away. *So, what if he* is *lifting my skirt? I don't want to resist. I only want to be as close to Josiah as possible.* He switched from one nipple to the other, and Annie moaned.

"Let me, sweet Annie," he murmured against her breast, "say yes."

"Oh, Josiah," she moaned. He reached under her skirt and cupped the apex of her thighs, where her hot, delicate flesh throbbed and ached in anticipation. He slipped her panties aside, parted her virgin lips and delved through, touching her wetness. Just as she had suspected, he possessed a natural affinity for sex, and she opened her thighs, eager to experience more. One finger slid deep into her as the heel of his hand brushed against her clitoris, stimulating the sensitive nub.

"Ooooooh," Annie wailed in pleasure.

"Say yes, Annie," he urged.

"Oh, Josiah, yes!"

No sooner had the words left her lips than his fingers withdrew. He slipped her panties down and off, then his body covered hers again. She opened for him again and his penis touched her intimate flesh. She sighed in pleasure, all thoughts of white weddings forgotten. All she could think, feel, and want was Josiah. She felt his muscles flex in preparation for the plunge into her...

And then his weight disappeared from her body. Annie opened her eyes. *When did I close them?* A shadow stood between her and the late spring sunshine. It took several seconds for her to focus, and then...

"Grandfather?"

The wiry man tossed Josiah away as though he weighed little more than a kitten. The boy stumbled and fell to the ground.

"Hannah, cover yourself." He averted his eyes from her bare body.

Face burning, Annie shoved her skirt down over her bare legs and twitched her blouse back into place.

As she restored her modesty, Grandfather snapped, "Josiah, go to your room and wait for me. If you're not there when I arrive, you'll never be welcome in this community again. Do I make myself clear?" His voice sounded calm, but his eyes flashed like chips of onyx.

"Yes, sir," Josiah replied, struggling to his feet and racing up the hill to the compound.

"Well, Hannah?"

"Annie, please, grandfather," she reminded him.

"Never mind about that. What do you have to say for yourself, young lady?"

"That I love Josiah, and I want to marry him." Annie rose gracefully to her feet and met her grandfather's eyes with her own unflinching gaze.

He raised one eyebrow even as he frowned. "But you are not married to him. No one has asked the elders. You are also underage. I don't see an almost married couple. I see a young, naïve fool being seduced by a bad..."

"Stop it!" Annie snapped, humiliation warring with wounded disappointment. "I love Josiah. He's not bad. You've known him his whole life. You know the last thing he'd ever do is harm me." *We got carried away. Nothing more. It happens when people are in love. And we'll only be underage a few months. Why is he saying these things?*

"I have known him his whole life," Smith agreed in a tone that did not bode well for Annie's hopes. Something unpleasant squirmed in her belly. What I know is that there's something wrong with him, Annie."

She crossed her arms over her chest. "There is not."

"No?" He raised his eyebrows. "Then how did you give up on your chastity so easily? I know you, Hannah. You don't want this; a clumsy lay in the meadow. Is that what all your talk of waiting, all your leadership of your peers has amounted to? I'm disappointed in you."

Considering her grandfather's questions about her behavior, Annie flushed. *Yes, I've been vocal in the youth meetings. And now, here I am, caught rolling around in the grass like a hypocrite.* She shook some flowers from her hair to distract herself from her burning shame. "I've behaved badly," she said, casting her eyes at the ground. Then she met her grandfather's gaze boldly. "But it was my decision. Don't blame Josiah. After all, he's one-quarter angel. There must be more goodness there than bad. It was a mistake, a lapse in judgment, not a crime."

"I don't know," her grandfather replied, his dark eyes focused on the horizon. "Of all Nephilim, I would least have suspected Lucien of indulging in improper behavior. He's just been promoted to lieutenant because of his courage, strength and honesty, and yet he was the one who broke his vows, who brought his infant to us to raise. There is weakness in his line. It shows in his son."

"No!" Annie shook her head, rejecting his words. "Lucien is our hero. If anyone can save us, it's him. And there's nothing wrong with Josiah. He's just a young man, and he loves me."

"He's said so?" The old man raised one bushy eyebrow.

"Not yet," Annie mumbled, frowning.

"Annie."

"What?"

"He's not for you."

A chill sank deep into the girl, freezing her from the heart out. *Not for me? He can't mean that. He knows Josiah and I are meant to be together. Everyone knows that.* Annie's entire plan for the future crumbled like rotten boards. She inhaled a pained gasp. "Why am I here then?" she demanded.

Grandfather blinked. "What do you mean?"

There. Now I have his attention. "Since I was a child, you've prevented me from learning to fight. I assumed it was because I was supposed to be with Josiah, our future champion. You never intended that, did you?"

"No." His blunt admission felt like a stiletto to the gut.

"Then why am I here? What need does the order have of me? If I'm not for Josiah, and I'm not going to fight, maybe I should go to Billings and take teaching courses." She crossed her arms over her chest. *I should leave. Then, maybe Josiah would follow. We could forget about clerics, Nephilim and Succubi, and live like normal young people in love. I've heard that legally, outside the compound, eighteen is the age of maturity.*

"You mustn't leave, Annie." Grandfather grasped her arm earnestly, and his eyes grew distant as he spoke. "I don't exactly know why, but you must stay. For one thing, this is the best way I have to keep you safe from what's coming. But... there's something. Argh, why can't I grasp it?" He rubbed his forehead in frustration, frowning deeply before returning his gaze to Annie. "I don't have an answer, except that I just know if you leave, all is lost. Please, Annie. Please don't make Josiah more than all of us."

Nothing further needed to be said. He gave her a long, disappointed look and walked away. Anne sank down in the grass and wept.

* * *

Mr. Smith wiped a tear from the corner of his eye. *I've lost so much over the long decades of his life. My wife, Mary, with her beautiful golden hair. Our daughter Pearl and her husband Jacob. My grandson Jake. Annie is all I have left.* He hadn't lied to her. The partial vision he received so often when he looked at her made it clear. *She is the key to so many things I don't fully understand, but one thing is certain. The war is coming. There will be no avoiding it. What remains unclear is whether any of us will survive.*

Mr. Smith squeezed against the wall as a herd of teenage boys galloped past him, their sneakers thundering on the tile like hooves. As they passed, he heard one call to the other, "Race you for the assault rifle."

"You're on, dude," a second boy agreed. With a roar of adolescent exuberance, the pair shoved their way to the head of the pack and burst through the rough-hewn door into the courtyard.

Shaking his head, Smith reached the end of the corridor and turned left, eventually arriving at the apartment Josiah shared with three other young men. He found the green-eyed youth flopped on his bunk, his chin in his hand, looking out the window.

Mr. Smith cleared his throat and Josiah jumped to his feet. Every instinct the older man possessed urged him to put this overzealous puppy in his place. His hands itched, and his teeth clenched. "Well, Josiah," he said, his voice all but a snarl, "explain yourself."

"I don't think I can, sir. I didn't... plan to do that." The green eyes fixed on one white tile on the floor between them.

"Look me in the eyes, son, when you talk to me," Mr. Smith insisted, "or have you learned nothing in all the years you've lived with us?"

Josiah looked up. Smith suppressed a shudder. *What is it about those eyes that always makes me uncomfortable?*

The two men regarded each other in silence, weighing their words. At last, Mr. Smith spoke. "It was a mistake to take you in, Josiah. You should never have existed."

The young man ground his teeth. "I've always known you felt that way, sir. In fact, I'm surprised you haven't thrown me out."

"You're not of age," he tossed back lightly. *That truly is the only reason he's been allowed to remain.* "But I swear by heaven, Josiah Angelson, if you ever go near my granddaughter again, I will. It's over between you. Is that clear?"

Josiah's eyes widened. "Sir, no, please! I swear I'll never do anything like that again. I love Annie. Don't separate us. Please!"

"My decision is made," Mr. Smith's rage expressed itself in icy control. "Her safety is key to our survival. Yours isn't. You will leave her alone from this day forward. If I hear you've so much as said hello to her, you're done here."

Josiah closed his eyes and swallowed hard. "Yes, sir," he said softly, but Mr. Smith saw the flash of rebellious stubbornness in those unsettling green orbs. *This isn't over, and we both know it.*

* * *

Josiah peeked out into the hallway. *Empty. Thank God. I don't want to see the old bastard ever again.* Josiah tiptoed down to the right. Something tickled his cheek and he swiped his sleeve over impatiently. *Damn it, I'm not going to cry.* Another tear followed the first one instantly. Then another. Josiah drew in shaky, unsettled breaths as he made his way to the Naphil dormitory. I need my father. *He can help me understand what to do.* He threw open the door, desperate to speak with Lucien.

Empty. Josiah closed his eyes, his head falling forward against the wood, his shoulders sagging. *I forgot. Father's gone.* All the Nephilim had been sent out on a huge mission to eliminate a nest of Succubi in Los Angeles. Humiliated, heartbroken, and despairing, he'd been left completely alone.

Part III

Chapter 13

Las Vegas 1999

The Assassin crept from shadow to shadow, not as invisible as the Nephilim, but as undetectable as a highly trained human could be. The small figure crouched behind an abandoned blue sedan. The uniform concealing the identity was designed to resemble the ninjas of bygone centuries, but it was white, not black. Only a pair of brown eyes showed above the face mask.

The figure crept out from behind the car in hot pursuit of the heat shimmer that signified a half-angel on the hunt.

It was not strictly necessary for The Assassin to hide. In this strange town, a person dressed in a white ninja costume would attract little attention. Most passers-by would simply assume any strange costume was part of a stage show or publicity stunt.

Here in the desert, any shimmering on the city streets could be dismissed as tricks of the heat, or of the neon lights that altered the environment at all hours.

I'm fairly sure which Naphil I've been sent to assist tonight. The Assassin had been sent to help roust out a nest of Succubi hidden inside a brothel that masqueraded as a strip club. *Intelligence suggests at least five demonesses hiding inside the building. It's a lot for one Naphil to handle alone. He won't be thankful, but I have my orders.*

Arriving at the club, The Assassin slipped through the door, unnoticed by a burly, blond-haired bouncer with the bulging muscles. *Looks like he's been selected for show more than intelligence or skill.*

Inside the dim interior, The Assassin found it easier to track the shimmer past the dance floor, where three women and a Succubus twined their half-naked bodies around poles embedded in the floor and ceiling. The Naphil progressed through a beaded curtain, to a back room where men sat on chairs while naked girls squirmed and twisted on their laps. In the corner, one overweight Succubus soaked in the lust. So immersed was she in the spectacle of the lap dancers that she did not recognize the angelic being in front of her until it was too late.

The lights dimmed as the sword, cleverly concealed in the fluorescent lighting, thrust into her bloated belly. A shriek, perceived as the squeal of brakes by mortals, pierced the night.

Without pausing, the Naphil moved on, entering a doorway with a sign reading *employees only.* The Assassin sneaked through just as the door swung shut. Inside were five beds. In three of them, Succubi fed on the lust of men with whom they were copulating. These demonesses proved more alert than their friend had been, and they quickly abandoned their prey, converging on three sides of the angel warrior, claws and fangs extended.

The Naphil materialized. *Lucien. Just as I thought.* His sword flashed, but the wary, serpentine women dodged his parries, one distracting him while another took advantage to slash at him. *He's going to need help.*

The three men lay on the beds all but dead, drained of their life force by the Succubi. Lucien and The Assassin had been too late to save them... almost.

Pulling a short knife from the belt of the uniform, The Assassin quickly put the three drones out of their misery with a quick slash across their throats, then approached the continuing battle.

The angel was tiring, and so far, only one Succubus bled. As two engaged him from in front, the injured one sneaked in behind, attempting to hamstring him.

The Assassin flew into action, sliding across the polished wooden floor on soft-soled shoes and thrusting the dagger into the demon woman's spine.

She shrieked as she died, bursting into a fine spray of golden dust, and the other two stopped in their tracks, wondering what had happened.

That pause was all Lucien needed to finish them both.

He then turned towards the small figure before him, his eyes narrowed. "Why are you here, Assassin?"

"I never know the reason, Naphil. I go where I am sent and do what I can to help."

"I do not need help from a human."

The Assassin didn't point out that he was clearly incorrect, at least this time. *Enraging a semi-divine being is not a healthy thing to do.* "I'll just go then. Good luck, sir."

The Naphil nodded. The Assassin returned the gesture and muttered the words that would cause relocation.

Eyes closed against the dizzying sensation, The Assassin relocated. The artificial light of the city gave way to the burning red of the desert. At the edge of the Mojave, a silver travel trailer baked in the sun.

A small, red-haired woman with green eyes climbed down the stairs, a welcoming smile on her face.

"Oh, there you are, my dear." She wrapped her arms around the figure, "What news?"

"I've been with your Naphil. He's safe, as of two minutes ago."

"Oh, thank the Creator. And my son?"

"I saw him a week ago. He's angry and conflicted, but well enough."

"And you, little one?"

"Nothing to signify. Do you have anything for us, Sarahi?"

"Oh yes, so much. Come inside. I'll make you some iced tea and we'll talk. But take off that mask, love. It's much too hot for so heavy a covering."

Nodding, The Assassin followed the turncoat Succubus into the trailer.

* * *

Josiah aimed a shotgun and fired. *Finally, tall and muscular enough to take the recoil without reacting.* His peers had stopped growing years ago, and he'd finally caught up with them. The shot made impact just to the right of the bulls-eye and fanned out. *If that had been a Succubus, she'd be dead.* Though he had yet to see it himself, the older men said they dissolved in golden dust. *I can't wait to experience that someday. In a way, I'm grateful to the Succubi. Because I'm allowed to hate them, it takes the pressure off everyone else I hate.* Josiah pumped the shotgun and fired again, this time imagining Mr. Smith's head on top of the target. Direct hit. *Damned old man.*

Josiah closed his eyes against a sudden sting. *Annie. Sweet Annie. Now forbidden. I love her so much. I really didn't mean to seduce her in the meadow. I only wanted a kiss, but her touch, for the first time, set me on fire in ways I can't explain. I can sort of remember willing her to submit, but I didn't think she would do it. I never meant to hurt her, only to be as close to her as possible.*

He opened his eyes and turned to look at the window on the far side of the compound. The elder council's meeting hall. *There she is.* He could see her nimbus of milk chocolate curls bouncing as she pulled a musty tome down from a shelf. As she stretched, her slender shape strained her loose blouse. A sizzle of heat shot through his loins. Try though he might, he could not abandon his love for Annie. He desired her beyond sense, beyond reason. *Someday, somehow, I will have her, but first, I have to prove himself.* He returned his attention to the shot-riddled target. The hot sun beat down on his head, but a cool breeze wafted, bringing the scent of pine drifting over the compound. *Compensate for the wind. Steady yourself. Calm. Slow your breathing and heart rate. Focus.* Josiah's finger squeezed on the trigger. *That's for you again, Mr. Smith, with your damned self-righteous bullshit.* BANG! *And for you, Father. Never listen. You think you know it all.* BANG! *And for you, Mother, whoever you are.* His finger faltered. A rosy haze seemed to be dancing on the breeze. *Peter.* BANG!

* * *

Through the window, Annie heard the target practice. She hurried over, the book forgotten in her hand. *Watching Josiah handle that weapon with such skill is far more interesting than prophecies of the Incubus.* Even though she was training to be a teacher, later a leader of the elder council, for now, she was a young woman, more interested in boys than books. *This boy in particular.* His bicep bulged as he hefted the shotgun, and several shots exploded from the muzzle in rapid succession. Tattered remnants of paper flapped in the breeze. *He beat the hell out of the target. I wonder what he pictures when he shoots the gun. All the grand adventures he'll be having once he passed his qualification exams, no doubt.*

I wished the day would never come. It's excruciating watching him work and not being able to touch him. Even at this distance, she noticed a little bead of sweat rolling down the back of his neck. She smiled. Then her smile faded. Every night, some mad voice in her head urged her to creep down the hall to his bedroom and climb into bed with him, to finish what they'd started in the meadow. She blushed just thinking about it. Other boys had asked her to sit with them at lunch, or to walk with them in the courtyard in the evening. She'd turned them all down. *I don't foresee it changing in the future. I only love Josiah. For me, it's him or nothing. I'd rather be alone than replace him.*

A clashing sound drew her attention to the far side of the courtyard, where two young men sparred with blunted daggers. Back before she'd been forbidden *any* contact with Josiah or weapons, she'd been one of the best at hand-to-hand combat. In fact, the excuse for denying her access to the practice field was that her ability discouraged the boys. *She sighed. I want to remain part of the clerical order and do what I can in the battle we all know is coming, but I have to admit this is a very old-fashioned society.*

* * *

The black fire that barely illuminated the interior of the hive where Lilith resided also put out no heat. Naked demonesses shivered in the corners of the room, their emerald eyes gleaming like lamps as they converted the dim flame into useful illumination. On the bed, the long, pale body of the demon queen writhed. A low moan echoed from her full lips. Then she let out an extended hiss. Beside her, a drone screamed. His yell was cut off as her long talons crushed his throat.

"Mother," a Succubus who stood a safe distance from the range of those deadly claws said, "it's time."

"I know that, idiot," the demon snarled. "I've done this thousands of times." Dropping the drone, she bore down, her molars grinding together. One fang speared her lower lip and black blood dripped down her chin.

From the foot of the bed, a long-haired woman reached out and scooped up the tiny creature who had just emerged from Lilith's body.

"Hello, sister," she whispered to the infant, a tiny girl with a wisp of golden hair and glowing green eyes. "Welcome." She wiped blood from the baby's face and body with a towel and then wrapped the little one in a blanket.

"Well?" Lilith snarled.

"Another fine daughter," the Succubus said hesitantly. Lilith howled in rage and rose to her knees, swiping claws in the direction of her two daughters. The Succubus turned to the side, protecting the baby and receiving four deep gouges in her arm. Blood spurted from the wound and the Succubus clenched her teeth, but she did not cry out.

"Another girl? Always another girl!" she hissed in disgust. "For centuries I have tried for a son. Why can I not have one? When will the promised Incubus arrive?"

"Mother?" A sly voice emerged from the shadows, followed by a golden-haired demoness with a devious expression.

"Yes, Jezebel?" Lilith addressed her most loyal and dangerous daughter.

"Do you suppose we have misunderstood some part of the prophecy?"

"What do you mean?" When Jezebel spoke, Lilith always listened. That Salome knew. She cuddled her newborn sister to her chest and slipped from the end of the bed, withdrawing to a hidden alcove where she could eavesdrop without being seen.

"Just this," Jezebel replied. "I have seen something that gives me deep suspicion. I went to visit one of the sisters some time ago, and she was holding a child. She said she was seducing his father, but now

I wonder. Why would that have been necessary? We Succubi have powers and need no such petty tricks."

"His?" The demon queen's voice emerged low and dangerous.

"Yes. A baby boy with the most striking green eyes, and then..."

"Go on," Lilith urged, her forked tongue lapping at her dry lips.

"More recently, when we attacked a family of clerics, they had with them the most amazing boy, with green eyes and a taste..." her own tongue shot out as though sensing the memory of the boy's flavor in the air. "It was like a Succubus... but not. He relocated instantly, and we never could find him again, but I couldn't help wondering what he was."

Salome gulped.

"Why did you not report this to me immediately?" Lilith asked. From her hiding place in the corner, Salome flinched. If Mother had used that tone of voice with anyone else, it would have been a precursor to a swift and bloody death.

"I didn't know what I was seeing. I didn't want to bother you if it turned out to be nothing. Since then, I've been poring over our library." She waved a clawed hand at a messy jumble of books and scrolls tossed haphazardly in and around several niches carved in the stone wall. "The more I study the prophecies, the more convinced I become that it does not refer to you as mother of the creature, but as an ancestor. Just suppose," Jezebel continued, "the Incubus had already been born, not to you but to one of your daughters..."

"Who?" Lilith demanded.

Salome did not wait to hear the answer. Tucking the baby safely into the cradle she'd placed in the alcove centuries ago, she vanished.

* * *

Josiah sat upright in bed, panting. The darkness of the boys' dormitory pressed in on him like a physical touch. *What on earth is wrong with me?* He felt... dirty, as though something disgusting had touched him in his dreams. He took a slow, deep breath and tried to remember. At first, the dream had been pleasant. The recurring image he'd had since early childhood. A softly touchable female figure in a soothing shade of pale rose, who glittered like sunlight on water, wrapped warm arms around him and sang. He loved those dreams, they always left him feeling great. But this time it had changed. The pink figure had turned a poisonous green and become snake-like. Cool coils, rough with scales, had replaced embracing arms, and a forked tongue had whispered scandalous suggestions in his ear before licking every inch of his body. Josiah gagged. *What's wrong with me? Why did I dream something like that*? He shuddered in disgust despite the arousal that still pounded through his body.

* * *

Sarahi stretched out under the orange sheet and buried her nose in the soft cotton. Twenty years since Lucien had been in this bed with her, and she still liked to pretend she could smell him there. She had hoped, after so long, her desire for him would fade and she would adjust to being alone again. She hadn't. The knowledge that her lover and her son were out there somewhere preyed constantly on her mind. She burrowed deeper under the sheets.

In the evening, temperatures dropped significantly, and she actually felt cold. *If only Lucien were here, his warm arms around me, his big body cradling mine in the darkness as we rest, sated and happy. And Josiah. My son is a man now, no longer a baby. He's grown, at last, to his full height. He hasn't quite reached his father's size, but he's tall by human standards. Broad shoulders, but thin and perhaps a bit gangly everywhere else. He looks more like an adolescent than an adult.* This surprised her as Succubi reached maturity in their early teens.

Sarahi let her eyes slide closed. I need sleep. *I can't afford to become exhausted. Too much rests on my ability to stay sharp. And maybe, in sleep, I can visit Josiah again.* Sarahi reached out with her senses, far to the north, where winter reigned over an undulating prairie.

Bang! Bang!

Sarahi jumped from the bed. *Who could be at the door*? For one crazy second, as she crossed the tiny length of the travel trailer, she dared hope her dark warrior would be there. Hope died as the light from the dim bulb above the entrance revealed her sister Salome. Black hair wreathed the medium brown skin of her naked body. Of all her sisters, this was one of the few she trusted... a little. All were loyal to Lilith, and therefore all were suspect, but Salome had some small affection for Sarahi, and had helped keep her out of trouble a time or two. That bought her a bit of leeway.

"Welcome, sister," Sarahi said warmly, indicating the interior of her trailer.

"No time. Sarahi, you have to get out of here now. Mother knows. She knows about your baby. She knows you betrayed her. She wants your head. Do you have somewhere you can go to hide? All the Succubi and drones will be after you."

Sarahi's stomach clenched. While she did not fear destruction, the death her mother would dish out to her was certain to be slow, agonizing and hideous. *But where can I go? What can I do? Is there a place on earth safe from Lilith's minions? If so, I'll never find it, not with all the hosts of darkness at Lilith's disposal.*

Stunned, Sarahi sank to the floor. *The best thing to do would be to end my existence myself, quickly, before they can find me.* Her heart cried out at the thought. *Never to see Lucien again, not even to say goodbye. Never to hold my son.* Despair too deep for tears rolled over her and she wrapped her arms around her knees and rocked.

"Sarahi, stop that! You have to go!" Salome tugged at her arm.

"Where will I go?" she asked, her voice flat and tired. "There's nowhere. It's over, Salome. Thank you for telling me. Now get out of here before she includes you in my punishment."

"You can't just give up!" Salome urged. "You have to keep trying. Please, Sarahi. You give me so much hope!"

Sarahi laughed bitterly. "Forget hope. We are damned creatures. There is no hope."

"You mustn't say such things," a new, fierce voice spoke from the doorway. Sarahi looked up to see the white uniform of The Assassin framed in the cheap aluminum doorway.

"I know you," Salome said, her narrowed eyes fixed on the slender figure.

"Of course, you do. I've spared your miserable existence more than once, demon."

The two glared at each other for a moment, then Salome shook herself. "Well, if you care anything for Sarahi, help me get her out of here. Do you know a place where she can hide?"

The Assassin's shoulders relaxed. "As a matter of fact, I do. Help me lift her."

Two sets of arms wrapped around Sarahi's torso and hauled her to her feet. Then the white-clad Assassin muttered a series of words in a language Sarahi couldn't understand and the world dissolved in a swirl of rainbow-colored light.

Chapter 14

One Month Later

Lucien stalked into the compound. He'd been gone almost two months, ferreting out a massive cell of Succubi and drones in Atlantic City. The battle had been one of the most horrific he'd ever seen. Even with the combined efforts of the seven Nephilim, four young clerics, and The Assassin, it had taken everything they had to be rid of those damned snake-women. If one of the drones hadn't turned on his Succubus, all might have been lost.

Miraculously, the entire group had survived the battle, but they were far from unscathed. Peter, the youngest of the clerics, had been hit hard over the head. The medics feared a concussion. They'd be keeping him overnight. Jim, a stout cleric on his last mission, had broken his arm. It was already set and bandaged, and the wiry, graying soldier wanted nothing more than to take some heavy-duty pain pills and sleep. The rest of them were all marred with bruises and scratches, many of which had required stitches. Lucien himself felt exhausted, as though he'd been bled out.

Inside the compound, the warriors instantly became alert. Jonas pulled his sword from its sheath with a resounding ring as he scented the air, eyes narrowed in concentration. Lucien inhaled, and a familiar tang touched his tongue. *Like a woman, but stronger, sweeter, more intense. I know that smell all too well.* He reached for the slender blades strapped to his back. The clerics, reacting to the actions of the Nephilim, pulled their guns.

"What?" Mr. Smith asked, taking them down the hall to the conference room for a short debriefing. At least, Lucien hoped it would be short. *I want to sleep more than I want to talk.*

"Mr. Smith," Jonas said, placing his hand on the elder's arm, "it feels like... it can't be... is there a Succubus in the compound?"

Mr. Smith sighed. "Yes, friends, there is. She came to us a month ago, begging for sanctuary, and she's been providing us with information about the hive. She isn't harming anyone."

"What is she eating?" Lucien asked, earning him puzzled stares from Nephilim and clerics alike. *Oh, that's right, I didn't share that bit of information with everyone.* "Succubi do not seduce merely to gain power. It is how they feed," he said succinctly.

Mr. Smith nodded. "That's right. She promised not to... seduce anyone, and thus far she has not. I have no idea how she's sustaining herself, but there have been no complaints. Try not to kill her, gentlemen. She's our best source of inside information about our enemy."

"If you can trust her," Jonas said, sheathing his sword grumpily. "The way I feel, she'd better stay out of my way if she wants to live."

The others nodded in agreement and Mr. Smith opened the door of the conference room, indicating they should enter.

* * *

Lucien rolled over in the bathtub and groaned as the hot water hit another scrape. *What's wrong with me that I'm losing focus? How long has it been since I could hold my own against a dozen Succubi or drones and walk away without a scratch? Am I getting old? No. Nephilim stop aging at around sixty years, the human equivalent of thirty or so. I should remain in my prime indefinitely unless I'm killed. So, what's going on?*

It was like in the last... ten years, since he had been released from the monastery, he hadn't cared if he lived or died. *But that's stupid. I have so much to live for.* Josiah had finally reached adult size and joined the ranks of the clerics, though the eager boy seemed to have given way to a sullen, joyless young man. Lucien had no idea how to reach him. The time he spent tracking down nests of Succubi meant less time to spend with his son. *I know Josiah resents my absence, but what else can I do?*

Lucien had arrived late the previous night and fallen into an exhausted slumber, only to awaken stiff and sore. So now he stretched out in this bath. As usual, his mind wandered to Sarahi. *What is she doing? Is she still alive? I've heard nothing one way or the other. No reason to think I would.* He'd been back to her trailer several times since his release from the monastery. He never approached, just stood nearby watching over her, inhaling her fragrance on the wind. Several times she'd been joined by The Assassin, the mysterious warrior in the white uniform. Lucien ground his teeth, fiercely reminding himself that she needed to feed. His stomach turned at the thought of her lying under another man. Year after desperate, lonely year he'd suffered in deprivation. *This is what she is. I can survive forever without sex. She can't.*

Savoring the cooling water one last moment, he rose, rivulets running down his bulging muscles, his scarred skin. Just the thought of his lady had brought him to raging, aching fullness. He considered taking care of it, but as the cold air hit him, the problem resolved quickly. He pulled on a pair of black jeans and a matching sweater, only slightly darker than his own skin, and looked in the mirror. He looked like shades of midnight brought to life. His shaved head gleamed under the glow of the light bulb above the sink. His eyes glittered. He had a new scar, one that angled across his forehead, down his nose, and cut into one cheek. It had been a nasty injury, one that had almost claimed him. *A scar is not the worst possible outcome.* Shrugging at his reflection, he left the bathroom, exited the Nephilim dormitory, and headed down the hallway to the council chamber. The elders would be waiting for his latest report.

* * *

Sarahi leaned against the door of an apartment. Inside, a couple was kissing in anticipation of making love. She could feel their rising desire. *Not lust. This is different. Cleaner. There's no guilt associated with their coupling. No dirty thoughts.* The woman sighed and then giggled. Sarahi's superhuman hearing could perceive the soft rustle as they undressed. *They'd be embarrassed if they knew I was here.* No one realized, in the month she'd been here, what she was. No one but the elder council, and they had cautiously agreed to this on the condition no one be harmed. Rather than taking a full feeding from a single couple every six weeks or so, she snacked about once a week, never taking more than the people could afford to lose. She sighed. A soft moan filtered through the door and the energy level rose. *I know them.* Young and eager, they'd been married less than a year. Recently enough that they wanted to sneak off during the morning break for a private moment.

I can remember the sweetness of love. She closed her eyes and imagined herself stretched out on the bed with Lucien's beautiful body pressed on top of her. She reached out with her senses. *He's been in this place. I can smell his scent, can feel his energy. I can almost taste him.* She inhaled deeply and the sense of him grew stronger... and stronger. Sarahi's eyes flew open just in time to see a tall figure striding down the hallway.

Her jaw sagged. His eyes fell on hers and he stopped in amazement. "Sarahi?"

"Lucien." She took a hesitant step in his direction, then stopped, too shy to move on.

"What... why... what are you doing here?"

"Hiding," she replied, letting her auburn lashes fall over her eyes.

"From what?"

"From Mother. She found out...everything."

He took a step towards her, close enough to touch. But he didn't touch. He looked, and she looked back.

"You are the Succubus who sought sanctuary with the clerics? Am I dreaming?" he demanded at last.

"If you are, I'm having the same dream," she replied.

Outside, a cloud rolled away from the sun, and the shaft of light falling through the windows illuminated a line that slanted diagonally across his face. Sarahi caught her breath. *An inch deeper and he'd be dead.* She reached out and trailed one hesitant finger along the ragged scar, her lip trembling, and her hand unsteady.

At last, he moved, faster than even her eyes could perceive, enfolding her in his arms and lowering his mouth to hers for a kiss of devastating power. He kissed her so hard it hurt, his lips mashing hers. She threw her arms around his neck and all but strangled him.

"Oh, my love," he murmured against her mouth.

"Lucien. How I've missed you."

From around the corner, soft footsteps approached.

"Come on, darling," she said, slipping from his embrace and taking his hand. Like children, they ran down the hallway to her room. Well, really, it was an unused storage closet. Most adults shared, but no one wanted to bunk with a Succubus, so they'd cleaned out this windowless ten by twelve-foot space and tossed a twin bed in it. It was to that bed which Sarahi led her lover. They tumbled to the mattress, making the springs whine in protest. There was no room to lie side by side, so Sarahi pushed Lucien to his back and straddled him, her long skirt bunching up over her thighs. She took his face in her hands and lowered her lips to his again. This time the kiss was less painful, though no less intense. Twenty years of separation flowed between them.

"I love you," she whispered.

"And I you," he agreed, lifting her loose white blouse over her head. His hands went to her hips, holding her still and upright on his belly. Her soft pale skin blushed with desire. She reached behind her back and unhooked her bra, baring her luscious breasts to his gaze, to his touch. This time he didn't need to be urged. He grasped one full mound in each hand. Then he urged her down over him again, so he could suckle her.

"Ahhh," Sarahi sighed as his clean, fresh-tasting desire flowed through her, filling her belly and moistening her sex at the same time. She tried to reach between their bodies and unfasten his jeans but couldn't.

"Let me up, love," she urged.

"What? Why?" His voice was dark with desire.

"I want you naked. Show me that beautiful body, Lucien."

He released her, and she rose, opening the tie of her skirt so the fabric pooled around her feet. In a pair of lace panties, she watched as Lucien stood and stripped off his shirt and jeans. He held out one hand to her and she stepped close. He enfolded her in his arms, and Sarahi felt safe for the first time in twenty years. This time when she slipped her arms around his neck and drew him down, it was for a delicate, sophisticated kiss.

How long they stood mostly nude in each other's arms, neither knew, but they took their time savoring the moment.

At last Sarahi could wait no longer. Her hunger sated, her desire began flaring out of control.

"Now, Lucien. I need you now!" she begged.

"Yes, love, I know." His hands went to her waist, skimming the scrap of lace to the floor and leading her back to the bed. She urged him down and straddled his narrow hips. There was just enough clearance on either side of him for her knees. He guided her, one hand on her hip, the other holding his erection into position, and she sank down, taking him deep.

"Oh! Oh!" she gasped, her head falling back. Her sunset hair swept his legs. He still, always, filled her like no other. He urged her to move, to ride him. She took over the movements, thrusting her body over his massive shaft. His hands went back to her breasts, pinching her nipples gently.

Reunion sex, she reflected in the tiny part of her brain that was still functioning rationally, was bound to be quick, and this time was no exception. Already her sex fluttered on the brink of orgasm. She wanted it, but not yet... *no, not yet...*

"Oh yes!" she wailed as pleasure wracked her. Her body writhed, sinuous and serpentine as pleasure rolled over her. Lucien grasped her, stilling her wild movements so he could drive up into her repeatedly. Each hard thrust brought her a new wave of exquisite spasms, and he held her still and made her take it all, every thrust, every inch, until her wails of ecstasy fractured into whimpering sobs.

Lucien drove deep once more and froze, groaning. Sarahi felt the flood of burning liquid in her core. They remained, trapped at the apex of pleasure, for a long moment. And then, at last, their bodies relaxed slowly until Sarahi lay limp on Lucien's chest, her head on his shoulder, his big hands on her back.

With the release of sexual tension came the release of self-control as well, and Sarahi's misery of the last two decades expressed itself in a flood of tears. Lucien stroked her hair as she wept on his shoulder. His hands felt so good on her. *I'd forgotten how good, but now I remember; now I feel alive again.* She savored his soft kiss on the top of her head.

"I love you, Lucien," she sniffled.

"And I love you, Sarahi."

"Never leave me again."

"As long as there is breath in my body, I will not, and that is a vow I shall never break."

Sarahi smiled through her tears.

Lucien's erection had softened inside her, but her needy body was far from finished with him. When he moved as though to withdraw from her, she placed her hand on the center of his chest and sent him a little pulse of energy. Instantly, his sex thickened to throbbing life. He groaned.

"How did you do that?" he asked her.

"Succubus," she replied with a flirtatious wink. He drew her down for a kiss, then stood, still sheathed inside her, and reversed their directions, bearing her down onto the mattress. Sarahi looped her legs over his elbows, presenting herself to him for another deep, thorough loving that left them both panting and sated.

Chapter 15

Lucien led his lady out of her bedroom. Much time had passed while they had been inside. He had missed breakfast altogether, and his stressed body was clamoring for food. She had taken a tremendous amount of energy from him. Not only the feeding, but the physical energy required for multiple orgasms had exhausted him, despite how wonderful it has been. Not to mention he'd just returned from a battle. Now he was starving to the point of lightheadedness.

Hand-in-hand they made their way through the compound to the empty kitchen. Lucien scanned the refrigerator and snagged an apple, crunching it noisily while Sarahi rummaged for a pan and heated it on the stove.

"How can a creature who does not need to eat know how to cook?" he teased.

"How can a creature sworn to celibacy be so good in bed?" she bantered back. He shut up.

Sarahi sautéed onion and bell pepper in the pan with some bacon, and then added a few beaten eggs. By the time he'd finished his apple and a banana, she'd completed the omelet and slid it onto a plate. Lucien devoured it. She sat beside him, toying with a cup of lukewarm coffee. While Sarahi did not require food or drink, she could ingest them if she so desired, or so she'd told him. Once the edge of Lucien's hunger was satisfied, he returned his attention to his lady, taking her hand and admiring the slender fingers, the perfect half-moon nails, and the silky soft skin. He touched his lips to her palm, and then to the pulse in her wrist. He felt her heartbeat increase. She opened her hand against his cheek, stroking him.

He stood abruptly and hauled her into his arms for another toe-curling kiss. *This is madness. We need to slow down.* But he couldn't.

"Sarahi!" A harsh voice behind them separated the couple.

Mr. Smith stood, arms crossed over his chest, regarding the Succubus with an angry scowl. "You promised us our men would be in no danger from you. You swore you'd never seduce them. What on earth is this?"

"Mr. Smith, I..."

"Quiet," he ordered, slashing the air with his hand. "You'll have to leave now. We can't have you here, not if you're harming our men."

"Moses," Lucien cut off the elder's tirade.

He stopped dead and turned, taking in the face. "Lucien? You? Did you learn nothing from your previous punishment?"

"Yes, as a matter of fact, I did," Lucien said, deliberately being cryptic.

"I know you have a... weakness for women, but a Succubus? Really?"

Lucien shook his head. "No, not in the way you think. Sarahi did not seduce me. She would not do that."

"But... but..." the cleric sputtered.

"Listen, you wanted to know... I'll tell you. This is not a casual encounter with a hungry Succubus. We've known each other a long time. Sarahi is... Josiah's mother."

That rendered the stuttering cleric silent. He looked from Lucien to Sarahi and back. *Apparently, my lady feels nervous.* She clung a little closer to him and he tightened his arm around her protectively.

"Mo... mo...mother?" Mr. Smith forced out at last. "You mean he's..."

"Half Naphil, half...me," she said softly.

"A demon," he gritted out. "That explains so much." A sour look passed over the elder's face.

"He's not a demon," Sarahi hissed. Lucien could not recall ever having heard that ugly, snake-line tone in her voice before. *Apparently, even a mother Succubus can be dangerous when defending her offspring.* "He's less demon than I am, and you let me stay here. What makes you dislike him so much?"

Smith snorted. "There's something wrong with the boy. And before you go all cobra on me, Sarahi, remember, I've raised him since infancy. You've never seen him. You have no idea the trouble he's caused in this place, with his strange urges and his unnatural abilities."

Her body tensed in Lucien's arms and he tightened his grip, silently warning her to remain calm.

"Listen, Mr. Smith," he said, "I've been here the last ten years, and I have not seen him behave differently than any of the other boys. Why are you so set against him? If this is the way you've treated him, no wonder he's begged me to take him away."

"I wish you had," Mr. Smith said coldly. "He should never have existed. I felt that when I thought he was your son by a human woman. Now that I know he's a demon..."

"He is *not* a demon," Sarahi repeated, more forcefully. "He is the Incubus, and you should be careful how you treat him. If he hates you, he will side against you. He'll go to *her.* Even now she calls for him."

Mr. Smith's eyes bugged out. "Incubus? But... that's just a legend!"

Sarahi turned in Lucien's arms, fully facing the furious elder. "If that's so, then why has Mother been trying to create one for millennia? She's not stupid. She knows the prophecies as well as you do—at least the ones she has access to. You have volumes here she's never seen. The Incubus exists. He lives right now. Where is he? Where is my son?"

Mr. Smith gulped. "He's been sent with several other junior clerics to investigate a Succubus in Billings."

Sarahi blinked.

"Now listen, ma'am, I think we need to talk."

"Yes, I agree," Sarahi said coldly. "I sent my son away, so he would be safe. If I hear he's been abused in some way..."

"He has never been harmed, I swear," Mr. Smith replied.

Sarahi tilted her head to the side, considering Smith. "Very well then," she said, though Lucien could tell from the tension in her arms that she wasn't fully convinced. "We *do* need to talk."

"We certainly do," the elder agreed. "In fact, let's gather the council, the other Nephilim, and the clerical generals. I think this is information everyone needs."

"I agree," Sarahi said. "That will give me a few minutes to gather my materials."

Half an hour later, the conference room was filled to capacity. The massive table seated two dozen, and the seven elders sat in a row on one side, with Mr. Smith at the corner, the seat of power. Opposite them were the generals of the Nephilim; Lucien, Jonas, and five others Sarahi did not know by name, though she'd seen them at one time or another. The rest of the seats were taken by the heads of the Order of Clerics; stoic men of whom Sarahi knew none. Younger clerics, teachers and elders-in-training crowded around the table, standing upright or leaning against the wall. Sarahi had been given a spot beside Mr. Smith, across from Lucien. Just as the meeting began, a silent figure dressed in white slipped into the room and found a spot in the corner.

All eyes turned toward Sarahi. She suddenly regretted volunteering to lead this discussion. After three millennia of hiding, she didn't like being thrust into the spotlight. And it really was a spotlight, the overhead bulb glaring down on her, leaving nowhere to hide. She gulped and met Lucien's eyes. He nodded, offering silent support.

"I wanted to start by thanking everyone who has made me feel so welcome here. It can't have been easy, having a Succubus in your midst." Gasps erupted all around the room and Sarahi suppressed a grin. *Ah, good. They're listening.* "The reason I'm here is that I've been marked for death by my mother. I don't know if you are aware, but all Succubi are the daughters of Lilith, in a literal sense. There is so much information I need to share with you. I'm not used to public speaking, so I hope you'll forgive me if I... ramble, and don't present my thoughts in the most organized way..."

"The demoness is your mother?" a heavyset elder demanded. "The Succubi are your sisters? Why did we not hear this before? And why are you turning against them? Have you no loyalty to your family?"

She turned to the man, meeting his eyes squarely, and he flinched. "You should be glad I have chosen your side," she told him coldly. "I choose to believe that DNA does not determine destiny. I have made a choice. Don't make me regret it." She let her nails grow from delicate, shell colored half-moons to become three-inch, razor-sharp talons.

He nodded once, cowed into silence.

"Now, does anyone else want to waste time on silly questions, or can we move forward?"

No one spoke.

She opened the book in front of her, an ancient text bound in musty-smelling leather. "All right. The information I wanted to present to you involves the Incubus."

Several people snorted, and one man near the door turned abruptly and walked out.

"It's a fact, not a legend," Sarahi announced. "He already lives."

That drew their attention back to her.

"What proof do you have?" Mr. Smith demanded. "You saying it doesn't make it so."

"You're right, and I'm prepared to offer it. I'm in a rather unique position, having spent my life with access to the library of prophecies owned by the Succubi. I've read them all. I never guessed the ones you had would be so... different. Combining them, I think I finally understand what they mean." She swallowed, glancing down at the book and then back up at the people around her, meeting their eyes. She locked gazes with The Assassin and received a wink. She smiled grimly. "What it means, friends, is that war is coming."

"I hate to break it to you, Toots," one of the cleric generals drawled sarcastically, "but we've been at war for millennia."

"I know that," Sarahi snapped. "I'm not talking about these little skirmishes and sneak attacks we've been engaging in since time immemorial. I'm talking about outright war. She will come, and she will kill us all."

"And just why would that happen?" the Naphil seated next to Lucien asked. "What reason could she possibly have to come against us now?"

"It's because of the Incubus," Sarahi said. "To the Succubi, to Lilith, it's not a legend or a myth. It's a fact. She's been trying for years to create one."

"Why?" Several difference voices posed the query simultaneously.

"Yes, that is the question," Sarahi agreed. "And that's where having access to both sets of prophecies has answered a lot of questions for me. Your records explain what an Incubus is. Lilith's explain what one does."

"Enough with the foreplay, Succubus," another of the clerics said. "Get to the point."

Sarahi rolled her eyes. *These people are infuriating.* "The point is; the Incubus is an inexhaustible source of power. He will not take energy from intercourse with others. He will create it."

"That's impossible," Mr. Smith said. "Energy cannot be created."

"Perhaps not as such," Sarahi admitted, "but it can be generated. Think of a static charge. When two objects rub against each other, it can create a spark, even if neither object is electrical in nature. That same kind of process goes on inside the Incubus."

She glanced around again. *They're finally paying attention. Good.*

"I believe I also know why. Our texts speak of the Incubus's power. He will be able to provide unlimited energy to his partner, or he can use it to enhance lust or even kill. He's a living weapon."

"I can understand why Lilith would want one," Lucien said. The sound of his deep voice made a little shiver roll up her spine.

"Yes. But what she did not understand was how to go about getting one. She assumed her demon blood, mixed with human, would suffice, if only a son could be conceived. But that's not the case. Human nature, tainted as it is with original sin, mixes easily with the demon. No conflict. No energy. It requires untainted DNA to create the friction which will result in the energy production."

"So, an angel, then?"

Sarahi looked for the source of the voice. It was a woman standing near the door.

"In a sense, yes. However, Lilith could rape an angel and not conceive. Their natures are too disparate. You might as well mate a tiger with a fish. Nothing would happen. The mingling requires a catalyst. Lilith herself can never produce an Incubus, because the catalyst, human DNA, is not present in her. She is fully demon."

She waited, hoping someone else would make the inevitable leap.

"So then," Mr. Smith said, "human DNA is the catalyst?"

"I believe so," Sarahi replied. "Because it is, as the scriptures say, 'God-breathed,' human can join with angel, as the existence of the Nephilim proves. However, because of sin..."

"Human DNA can also merge with demon, producing Succubi."

She nodded.

"So then," drawled one of the clerics, a young man with bright blue eyes and a lusty gaze, which raked insolently over Sarahi's torso, "spit it out. How do you make an Incubus?"

"Isn't it obvious, Peter?" Lucien asked the boy. "If the mingling of demonic and angelic blood can only happen in the presence of human DNA, then the way to produce an Incubus is..."

"To breed a Naphil to a Succubus?" The blue eyes widened. "Good thing Nephilim are chaste!"

Lucien's dark skin turned even darker. "Not entirely," he said in a tight, strangled-sounding voice. All eyes turned from Sarahi to him.

"Lucien?" Jonas said, his voice tight as though begging him not to go any further with this line of thought.

"You know I have a son. You all know this. It is not a secret."

"But Lucien... his mother is human," Jonas protested. "Tell me she's human."

"No," Sarahi answered. "Only half."

The implications sank in slowly. Eyes and expressions spoke of rejection, fear and revulsion.

"We've been harboring a demon in our midst?" one of the elders asked, disgusted.

"My son is not a demon," Sarahi said firmly. "He has the potential to be a great hero, our savior. If we can harness his power, we just might be able to destroy Lilith for good."

"And how do we do that?" Peter asked.

"From what I've read, the Incubus is like... a duck. He imprints to his first partner, and only that woman can connect to his energy. So, who would it be?"

She met eye after eye. Every person, each and every one, blushed and turned away.

"What?" she asked.

"It's just..." Mr. Smith started, then broke off, visibly steeled himself, and continued. "You mean sexual partner?"

"Of course."

As one they all turned their eyes to the floor.

"Would someone please explain the problem?" Sarahi insisted.

"Listen, love," Lucien said, "to the clerics, sexuality is... intensely private. To the Nephilim, a total mystery. You are speaking of this as though it were a casual coupling, as though it were nothing."

"Oh no," she said, "it's very important. I just need to know who."

"No one," Mr. Smith said. "He's unmarried."

"He's twenty-one years old," Sarahi said, incredulous.

"That's not so very old to be unmarried, here," Mr. Smith replied.

Sarahi didn't respond, but it occurred to her that being married meant a great deal to them. She'd never encountered an attitude like it. "All right, well there's no time to lose," she said after carefully measuring her words. "Even now, Lilith is searching for him. If she becomes his imprinted partner, we have no chance."

Now everyone was squirming.

"Imprint on Lilith..." Mr. Smith stammered, "but that means..."

"Try not to think about it," Sarahi urged. "But it's really important to prevent it. I'm sure you'll all agree."

"Well, that's a problem," Peter said. "There's only one girl he likes..."

"It will never happen," Mr. Smith said firmly.

"What now?" Sarahi demanded.

"Josiah's crazy about Smith's granddaughter," Peter said irreverently, earning him sharp glances from all the elders. "Has been forever."

"And so?"

"So, I won't have that demon child near Annie," Mr. Smith said. Sarahi raised her eyebrows.

"I'm afraid a lot of parents are going to feel the same way," a female elder said, having the good grace to look apologetic.

"I see," Sarahi said. "Harnessing an unlimited source of energy means nothing to you people?"

"There's more to it than that, love," Lucien said. "These people set a great store by marriage. Josiah has been raised by them. He is... quite attached to Annie. I doubt he would consent to anyone else."

Sarahi shook her head. *Can they not understand?* "Every day he remains unmated, the risk increases. Lilith knows he exists. She will be reaching out to him, trying to tempt him."

"There is no way a child of our community would consent to incest, not even that one," Mr. Smith insisted.

"And if he has no idea the beautiful creature in his dreams is his grandmother?" Sarahi let the question hang in the air, daring someone to take it up. Only Peter spoke.

"No disrespect, ma'am, but I think you're overstating Josiah's importance. I've known the kid his whole life. He's weak, small. Barely equal to the lowest cleric, let alone some otherworldly creature. I really doubt he has the capacity to be... all that you say."

"Peter, be quiet," The Assassin snapped in a raspy whisper. "You're an overrated, self-centered turkey. This is no time for your egotistical bullshit."

The youth colored and shut his mouth with a snap.

Sarahi grinned at her friend and winked.

"We will consider the situation," the female elder said in a pompous tone, "but I don't expect this to be resolved quickly. Is there something we can do in the meantime to help ensure our safety?"

"Yes," Sarahi said. "Bring my boy home. I want to see him, and if he's here, we can work on finding him a wife, since that's so important to you people."

"It is," Mr. Smith said softly.

It looked as though the meeting was about to break up when Jonas spoke. "What about Lucien?"

"What about him?" one of the elders replied.

"His lover is here; the mother of his child. There's no way he can maintain his vows in the face of that. I wouldn't be surprised if they'd been fornicating already."

Lucien blushed, giving away the answer. Sarahi nailed the Naphil with a green-eyed glare.

"Well, Lucien, have you broken your vows again?" Mr. Smith demanded.

"He hasn't," Sarahi insisted.

"Liar," one of the elders accused, pointing a gnarled finger in Sarahi's direction. "Are you denying you've been intimate?"

"Not at all," Sarahi replied lightly. Across the table, Lucien choked. "I'm saying it was no violation for him to do so."

"How do you figure?" the elder asked.

"Well, he broke that vow long ago, right?"

The old man nodded.

"Did he ever remake it? Lucien, did you swear, after your return, that you would never touch a woman again?"

"No," he replied. "I knew you were out there somewhere. I would never swear a vow I knew I could not keep. Luckily they never asked."

"There you see," Sarahi said, her voice filled with triumph. "He never vowed. He's free."

"Hey!" Peter protested. "Why should he get to have a hot woman to play with? Shouldn't our heroes have to follow the same rules we do? I can't have a girl in my bed until I get married, right? So why does he get to?"

Suddenly, everyone was talking at once. Lucien brought one big hand down on the table. The shouting ceased.

"This is not my decision to make. However, I will not be parted from Sarahi again. From this day forward, I go where she goes. I fight only for her."

Sarahi's jaw dropped. "Lucien," she whispered into the tense hush, "you don't need to do that."

"I do," he said. "I love you."

Sarahi felt prickles of heat climbing up her cheeks. Her eyes burned with tears and her throat clogged. "Oh, Lucien," she said softly.

"Very well then," Mr. Smith said, "since you obviously won't stop your wicked ways, and we can't have you setting a bad example for everyone, you two will be married this afternoon. If you refuse, you'll both be cast out. We'll figure out how to deal with your... child later."

"I'm agreeable," Lucien said.

Sarahi nodded, not trusting her voice.

"Wait a minute," Jonas said, "that's worse. I want a wife. I bet there's not a Naphil at this table who would say otherwise. Why should Lucien get one?"

"They've already born a child together," one of the female elders pointed out.

"I can make that happen," Jonas said, arching an eyebrow. The other Nephilim were nodding.

"Gentlemen, wait," Mr. Smith said, "are you saying you *want* wives?"

"Yes, Mr. Smith."

"But, Jonas, why didn't you ever say anything?"

"We did, many times. We have always longed for that connection. You clerics made celibacy a condition of your help. We gave up asking centuries ago."

"I beg your pardon," Mr. Smith said, contritely. "I had no idea. I assure you it was never my intention to deny your people such an obvious need. Remember, when we came of age, rose among the clerics, you were already established, with your rules, culture, everything. I assumed you took those vows as a formality." The man looked flabbergasted. Sarahi couldn't take it anymore.

"But that's foolish," she interjected.

"What do you mean, Succubus," he asked her coldly.

"I'm sorry, but think, sir. Where do Nephilim come from?"

"From the joining of angel and human," he replied as if by rote.

"Have you ever considered what that means?" she asked, tilting her head to the side.

"What?"

"That the angels *lay* with those human women. Why on earth would the joining of two sexual beings create an asexual one? That makes no sense."

His eyes nearly bugged out of his head. "Why didn't I think of that?" he muttered.

"Perhaps because you're not a Succubus," she said with a gentle smile.

"Well, this is a dilemma," Mr. Smith said.

"I don't think it is," Lucien disagreed. "Give them the same rules as clerics. If they want a wife, they can have one. She must be at least twenty years of age and give full consent. And gentlemen, there are no divorces in this society, so if you choose badly, you're stuck with her. Also, we're ageless. Human girls are mortal. If you marry, you'll watch the woman you love age and die." Lucien reached across the table and took Sarahi's hand. She stroked her thumb over his fingers. "That should be enough reality to keep you from making foolish decisions."

"If your lady is right and that demon is coming for us," Jonas said darkly, "we might all be dead in short order."

"If we can keep Josiah on our side," Sarahi replied, "we just might stand a chance."

Sensing she was finished, the clerics and Nephilim began to drift away.

Sarahi rose and circled around the table to Lucien. He wrapped his arm around her slender waist and leaned down to kiss the top of her head.

"Mr. Smith," she turned to address the elder once more.

"Yes?" he asked warily, clearly not recovered yet from the events of the day.

"When does my son return? I need to see him."

"We're expecting them any minute," he replied. "I'm surprised you didn't ask about him sooner."

"I had no idea he was here," Sarahi explained. "When The Assassin brought me, she just told me I would be safe. She never said a word about Josiah."

"She?" Mr. Smith raised his eyebrows.

"Yes. The Assassin is a girl," Sarahi replied, "but she's never told me her name, so don't ask me who she is."

"Well at any rate," the elder went on, "I don't know when the young clerics will return, but you two are going to be married this afternoon, before you incite a riot. Sarahi, go to the storage room next to your room and look through the white dresses. There should be one you can wear."

Sarahi nodded.

"And is it too much to ask the two of you not to... do it until after the wedding?"

Sarahi gave him a wicked smile that set his cheeks aflame but said nothing. Lucien pondered the question. "I think we might just be able to manage... if you hurry."

The elder hurried all right. He nearly ran from the room.

"Just what is it about me," Sarahi asked as they walked, hand in hand down the hall, "that makes everyone so uncomfortable?"

"Well, love, you represent the decadent lifestyle a lot of them secretly wish they had experienced."

"But, Lucien, I hated that."

"I know, love. If you truly were a tramp, I wouldn't have wanted you."

She grinned. Then her smile faded. "Does it bother you how I used to live?"

He scoffed. "Sarahi, it's two millennia past. And it's not as though you had a choice in the matter."

She nodded.

"I love you. The rest doesn't matter to me."

That made her smile. "Now if only we can figure out how to get Josiah and this Annie together, all will be well."

Lucien faltered a bit.

"What?" she asked him.

"Doesn't it feel... I don't know...awkward to talk about sex that way?"

"No," Sarahi replied, genuinely puzzled by his response. "No more than you would feel awkward talking about what you had for dinner last night."

Lucien pondered for a moment. "Why is it," he said, "that Josiah lives on food like a human or a Naphil. Why doesn't he need to be fed your way?"

Sarahi considered. "I suppose because he's only one-quarter demon. It's not a strong part of his nature. He's more human than anything else." She tapped her thumbnail against her front teeth. "Are you sure he doesn't, though? There's a lot more to this than what I told them at the meeting."

"What, love?"

"He has all the powers of a Succubus, but in male form. He can enhance lust in women. That means, if he isn't careful, he could become quite a seducer. Even a predator. Maybe it's good such a repressed group raised him. If he doesn't imprint properly to a good girl, he'll become a monster in his own right. In Mother's hands..." Sarahi shuddered. "Mr. Smith needs to get over hanging onto his granddaughter. All our lives might just depend on it."

"I know, love, but I don't know how to fix it. He's a good leader, but where Annie's concerned, he's just not rational."

They arrived at the storage room and Sarahi entered, Lucien following closely behind. It was a long rectangular room filled with cast-off clothing. Each wall had a bar installed at shoulder height and one at hip level. Two rows of silver racks stretched the entire length of the room. In the compound, nothing went to waste. Just inside the door was a basket of clothing too worn out to be handed down, ready to be converted into rags and patches. Overhead, a single low-watt bulb provided only the dimmest illumination, just enough for her to find the white dresses. They were all the same; long and shapeless, and she held one up.

"Do I really have to wear this?" She made a face.

"When in Rome," Lucien replied.

"Oh, oh, I know how that goes!" Sarahi chirped. "When in Rome... kiss an angel!"

Lucien raised his eyebrows. "Does that go for storage closets as well?" he asked.

"As far as I'm concerned, there's no wrong place." She walked into his arms. Just as she had expected, he crushed her in a tight hug.

"Jonas is right about one thing," he murmured against her lips.

"He was right about a great many things. Which one do you mean?"

"Times are uncertain. We have to be close to the ones we love."

"We do," Sarahi replied. "Starting right here, right now."

He pushed her through a forest of hanging garments up against the wall and kissed her breathless.

If anyone had been outside the closet when the two emerged, they would have noticed how unusually red Sarahi's lips looked, how pink her cheeks. They would also have noticed her towering half-angel walking with a decidedly uncomfortable gait.

As they reached the main entrance, there was a loud roar of shouting and thundering feet. A crowd of young men ran into the room and pounded down the adjoining hallway to where most of the bedrooms were located. *It appears the clerics-in-training have returned.* Sarahi scrutinized them, desperate to pick her son from the herd of youths, but they galloped down the hall and vanished. Behind them, a tired-looking Naphil dragged himself through the door and slammed it shut.

"By all the light of Heaven, I would rather face a nest of Succubi than babysit those young fools!" he said to no one in particular. "All they think about is glory and adventure."

Lucien chuckled, filled with good humor. "Can't you remember being that young, Phillip?"

"Lucien! You're back! No, I was never that young."

"No?" Sarahi could hear the amusement in Lucien's voice. "So, I never had to pull you out of a nest of reveling Japhethites and Succubi?"

"Of course not," Phillip said, flashing his gleaming teeth. "What's been happening around here?"

"Amazing things," Lucien replied, a wide smile spreading across his dark face. Sarahi's heart turned over. *I'm actually going to* marry *him!* "You'll never believe it."

"Well, spill," Phillip urged. "I want to get a spot in the shower before those wild beasts use up all the hot water."

"They've rescinded the vow of chastity for Nephilim!" Lucien exclaimed. "We will be expected to live by the same rules as any other cleric. I..." he stopped, then pressed on. "I'm getting married this afternoon."

At last, it appeared the Naphil noticed Sarahi. He focused his gaze on her and blinked.

"Hello," she said. "I'm Josiah's mother."

He blinked some more. "Congratulations," he said. And then he staggered off down the hallway in an obvious state of shock.

"Love, which bedroom is Josiah's?" Sarahi asked. "I need to see my son."

"Come on," he told her, leading her down the hall and opening the door of one of the dormitories.

"This is the room Josiah shares with three other young men."

Sarahi looked at the four identical beds. Her hands began to tremble.

"Do you want me to stay?" he asked her.

She shook her head. "Go get ready."

He nodded and kissed her softly before leaving the room and shutting the door.

Sarahi sat down on the bed and waited.

* * *

Josiah walked down the hallway towards his bedroom, pulling a sweater over his head as he went. Fighting had been exciting, disturbing, and exhausting. Now all he wanted to do was take a quick nap. The other boys had galumphed off to the kitchen in search of snacks, but Josiah wasn't particularly hungry. As always, his thoughts turned to Annie. *I wonder if she likes teaching the little ones, if she's happy with her studies. If anyone has caught her interest. If she ever thinks about me.* He still didn't understand what had happened that day in the meadow. The event had never been repeated, but when he had seen a real live Succubus for the first time last week, something inside him had responded to her in ways he had not expected. *She was beautiful. Of course she was, but it was more than that. She had a magnetic pull. It resonated through me like a gong.*

Josiah shook his head. *If Father is finally home, I'll ask about it later. The other boys denied feeling it, so maybe it's a Naphil thing.* He opened the door and blinked in surprise.

A beautiful woman with long red hair sat on his bed. Upon seeing him, she rose to her feet, tiny and graceful, and walked across the room until she stood directly in front of him.

"Josiah," she said.

"Do I know you, ma'am?" he asked.

Don't you? The voice sounded in his head. He tilted his head and looked at her again. *I'm sure I've never seen her before, and yet she seems... familiar.*

He closed his eyes and a fragrance wafted over him. Again, he could almost swear he'd smelled it before; like cactus flowers, night blooming jasmine, and something else less easily defined.

"Rose," he said without thought, and then opened his eyes.

She frowned at him with a puzzled expression. "Where did that come from?"

"I don't know," he said. "Something about you just seems... pink. Enough games. Who are you and why are you in my room?" He hadn't meant to sound so gruff, but the presence of this woman caused the strangest sensations to well up inside him.

"Pink." She grinned. "That's what your father always said. Josiah, my name is Sarahi. I'm your mother."

Mother? Josiah closed his eyes again and reached out with those inexplicable senses he seemed to have. *Yes, that's the scent I recall from my dreams, when the sparkling pink woman holds in her arms and whispers words of love and encouragement that leave me feeling renewed for hours or days afterward.*

"Have you been in my head all this time, in my dreams?" he asked.

"Yes, Josiah. I've never left you." She wrapped her arms around him for a warm hug. In his dreams, she'd been big, a mother to his child. But he was adult-sized, over six feet tall, and her petite body felt child-like. He hugged her back.

She sniffled. "Can you ever forgive me, darling, for leaving you all these years? I had to do it, but I hated it every day."

"I..." He started to give a neutral answer, but that dream-scent washed over him again. It seemed to be coming from her hair. The rational part of his mind told him it was just shampoo, but the power of her aroma finally overwhelmed his overwrought, exhausted nerves.

"Mom," he said, and his voice broke. He crushed her in trembling arms and struggled not to break down completely.

His mother had no such reservations. She wept unabashedly in his embrace. "Look at you, darling," she said, her voice a little broken. "I'm so proud of you."

"For what, Mother? Growing up? I sure took my time about it."

"You're a unique creature, Josiah." Sarahi wiped her eyes and met his gaze. "Who knows how one such as you should grow?"

"That's what Father said," Josiah replied.

"And he was right, wasn't he?"

Josiah made a face but nodded.

"What?" she asked him. "Was he not a good father?"

"He's all right, I guess. But he thinks he knows everything. And he never listens. Sometimes it makes me really mad."

"I'm sure," she said. Then she smiled a funny little half-smile. "You know, I never had a father. Not really a mother either. My sisters took care of me when I was little. It seems to me that having a father, even one who doesn't do everything perfectly, is still better than no father at all."

She was right. Josiah knew it, but he didn't want to admit it yet. He gave his mother one last squeeze and stepped back. "I'm really glad you're here, Mom. I've wanted to meet you. I have so many things I want to know about you, about where I came from and who you are and... everything." *About what could be so dangerous that you had to be separated from your child for two decades, to start with!* "But it's a little... overwhelming right now. Would it be okay... could I have some time to... to kind of take it all in? Figure out how I feel?"

The woman blinked. "Yes, of course, Josiah. I'm not surprised you need a moment's peace. When you're ready, let me know and I will answer any question you have. I have something I have to do right now, but come and find me when you're ready and we'll talk, okay?" She pulled him down and kissed his cheek. "I love you, Josiah."

She smiled, the kind of smile that warmed hearts whether they wanted it or not, and turned to go, waving at him with two fingers as she walked out of the room. Josiah sank heavily onto the bed. *When I got home, I felt exhausted, worn out and grumpy. Now I'm also confused.*

* * *

Sarahi stepped into the hallway, shut the door and leaned against it. *Soon I'll have to meet Lucien and Mr. Smith in the chapel. That will be... amazing, but seeing Josiah is better. I can see he's conflicted, and no surprise. The child in him still feels the sting of abandonment, no matter how necessary, and of course, he doesn't really understand yet why it was so important. I wonder if he knows I'm a Succubus. Likely not. That will be another revelation, and he's so confused already. I can feel a deep resentment and animosity radiating from him. Not toward me exactly, or at least not entirely. My boy is disenchanted about a great many things, if his obvious rage is any indication. Part of it, I suppose, is a young man's angst. Based on what I've heard so far, it's not entirely unjustified. It sounds like he'd faced systemic prejudice in this place throughout his whole life, and that was before they found out he's one-quarter demon. His loyalty to the Order of Clerics is far from secure. He needs a strong tie to someone in this place or he could still be lost, and neither Lucien nor I will be the one to provide that bond. Parents never are.*

While she had been standing there, several people had passed in one direction or the other, intent on various tasks. Some of the men had eyed her curiously, making her smile. A few women had given her an ugly look, which she'd ignored. But a passing figure made her wandering thoughts gel into a sudden, radical decision. "Annie?"

The white-clad person stopped and turned. Sarahi grinned. *My suspicion was correct. The Assassin, the masked warrior the clerics trust without knowing her face, or even her gender, is also the girl my son loves. My hosts will hate me for what I'm was about to do, but the stakes are too high for squeamishness.*

"Sarahi, hello," the young woman behind the mask said, not realizing she had just been outed.

"Take off that mask, please, Annie. I don't like to talk to people I can't see."

The girl scanned the hallway and, finding it empty, lowered her face covering.

"It's so good to see you, darling," Sarahi said.

"You too. How are you adjusting to this place?"

Sarahi shrugged. "Well enough, I guess. I don't think I'll ever really fit in here."

"Everyone is jealous of you." Annie grinned. "You have a freedom they lack."

"I'm about to give up that freedom for good," Sarahi smiled back. "They've decided Lucien and I need to marry immediately. In fact, I'm on my way there right now."

"Wow!" Annie's brown eyes widened. "Congratulations!"

"Thank you." Sarahi's smile spread until her cheeks hurt. Then she set her crafty little plan in motion. "I'm running late, and I need to get to the chapel about ten minutes ago, but I left something in the room over there. Would you be a darling and get it for me?"

"Okay," Annie agreed. "What is it?"

"You'll know it when you see it," Sarahi said.

Annie's desire for Josiah glowed so brightly, it amazed Sarahi that she'd never noticed it before. She sent a little pulse of enhancement energy into the girl, then she dashed down the hall before Annie could ask any more questions.

Sarahi opened a couple of wrong doors before she found the chapel. High on one wall, a small, round stained-glass window admitted a shaft of multicolored light. Two sections of red-cushioned chairs waited for Sunday service, but today they stood empty. Only Lucien waited at the front for her, and Mr. Smith stood behind the pulpit.

"The dress, Sarahi?" Mr. Smith questioned.

"Sorry. I misplaced it. Does it really matter?" she asked.

I suppose not. It's not as though anyone is under the illusion that you're a virgin, after all." He sighed. "Come on then."

She smiled and walked up the aisle to her lover, taking his arm, ready to make her own vows.

* * *

Annie stepped through the door without stopping to consider what room it was or what she might be looking for. Inside she came to a dead stop. Josiah sat on the bed staring at her with a stunned expression on his face. She hadn't so much as said hello to him since that disastrous day in the meadow three years ago, after Grandfather had forbidden it, but she had never forgotten him. *No one means as much to me as Josiah. No one.*

"Annie?" his eyes clung to her like a starving man regarding a juicy steak. "Why are you here, love?"

"I'm not sure," she said. "Your mother..."

His eyes grew wide and he gushed, "You met her? Isn't she beautiful?"

"Yes, Josiah, she is. We've been friends a long time."

He wilted. *And no wonder. So many people knew his mother before him.*

Josiah straightened his shoulders, drawing dignity around him like a cloak. "You should leave, Annie,"

"I know," she said. But she didn't leave. Instead, she stepped closer, drinking in the sight of him. Short, messy black hair that couldn't decide if it wanted to be curly or straight. Chiseled, angelic features. Glowing green eyes. Kissable lips she hadn't tasted in far too long. Bulky shoulders to which a thin black sweater clung enticingly.

"Annie, leave now."

"Yes. I'm going." She walked even closer, close enough to touch. Then she sat down on his lap and slid her arms around his neck.

"Don't do this, Annie," he warned. "I've tried to live by your grandfather's rules, to stay away from you, but my willpower is low right now. I'm tired. And… and I want you."

"I want you too, Josiah. Surely you know that." She kissed him.

"I thought you were mad at me," he said when she pulled back to breathe.

"Never. Why would I be?"

"The meadow. I wasn't thinking. Wasn't listening. I didn't mean to hurt or dishonor you, Annie."

"You didn't. I loved how you touched me. I didn't want you to stop. Do it again."

"Annie, if I touch you, your grandfather will throw me out."

"He won't. I won't let him. We're adults now. He has no right to interfere. I know what I want, Josiah. Touch me." She kissed him again and guided his hand to her breast. Then she pulled back and watched. His face twisted into a conflicted expression as he caressed her nipple. She saw the exact moment his resistance collapsed. They fell back on the bed, kissing and touching. This time, no seduction was necessary. Each was wild to have the other.

Josiah had Annie out of the white suit in a flash, faster than she'd even realized he was capable of moving. Finally free to do so, he explored her slender body, caressing her little breasts, kissing her with wild passion as he pressed against her with the weight of his body.

"I love you, Annie," he whispered. A thrill shot through her belly, part sexual arousal, part deep love. *How long I've wanted to hear him say the words. After Grandfather's ultimatum, I thought it would never happen. Now here I am, right where I want to be, naked in Josiah's bed.* She felt no shame, convinced this was meant to be.

"I love you," she whispered back.

She lifted his sweater over his head and pressed kisses all over his chest and shoulders. Josiah returned the favor, lifting her breasts in turn and nibbling and sucking the sensitive peaks. She sighed with pleasure. *He's a natural. Unless...* "Josiah, have you done this before?"

"Yes," he replied, and her heart plunged. "With you, in the meadow. You're the only woman I want."

He scooted down her body, cupping her hips in his hands and kissing her belly. Annie wasn't ignorant. She and the other girls had read naughty novels and giggled. She knew how this worked. But when his tongue parted her folds and lovingly lapped her, she realized her imagination had not been anywhere near accurate.

"Oh, Annie," he groaned, "you taste so good." He slipped one finger deep inside her. "All mine."

She arched her hips, urging even him to deeper penetration, but he slipped the finger out. She whined in protest and he chuckled. He pushed two fingers inside her, sliding them gently in and out while he kissed and teased her clitoris.

In no time, Annie was drenched and panting, poised on the brink of orgasm. Josiah didn't stop. He eased her over the threshold into that devastating peak, where she writhed in ecstasy. "More, Josiah," she begged. "Please, give me more!"

"Tell me what you want, Annie. Do you want me inside you?"

"Oh yes," she pleaded. "Yes, Josiah. It's right. Don't you feel it?"

"Yes, I feel it. Here, baby, feel this." He guided her hand down to his straining erection and Annie moaned, bending her knees and parting them wide. She stroked him a couple of times and then guided him into position. This time there would be no stopping. He rammed into her with a mighty thrust, claiming her body for himself.

Annie sucked in a sharp breath at the sudden pain, but it didn't stop her from lifting her hips to him, forcing him even farther inside. She wanted every inch to be filled by him. He moved forward until he was rubbing against her deepest place.

How he held off his orgasm, she didn't know, but Josiah was far from finished. He claimed her aching passage again and again, gliding through her wetness, pulling out, and surging in again. Her own arousal had been subdued by the sudden sting of his entrance, but as the pain faded his slow, deep thrusts began to build her pleasure again. *If it can feel this good when I'm so tender, the next time should be phenomenal.*

Josiah's thrusting grew harder and faster, bringing him quickly to his own peak. Annie stroked his back as he growled and ground his body against her.

As his erection waned, he slipped from her sore sex, and Annie whimpered a bit.

"Did I hurt you?" he asked, concerned.

"You took me," she replied, "and I was a virgin. Of course, it hurt, but I'm not sorry, this was what I wanted." She cuddled Josiah close in her arms and kissed his cheek.

"I took you because I love you."

"I let you because I love you."

Their lips met again.

"Your grandfather is going to throw a fit." He frowned.

"I know. Ask me if I care." Her fingers trailed down his back.

"You should. He only wants what's best for you."

"Let's not talk about him," Annie insisted.

Josiah nodded. "Tell me about this costume you were wearing when you came in. It's not Halloween. Are you really The Assassin?"

"Yes," she admitted. "They told me girls can't fight. I think I've proven them wrong."

One side of his mouth curled into the parody of a smile. "It's not that you can't. It's that people don't want to see you in danger."

She snorted. "Josiah, we're all in danger. Every day. Every hour. How am I in less danger if I don't know how to defend myself?"

He grinned. "You don't have to convince me. You've been better at this stuff than me from the very beginning."

"It's not a competition, Josiah," she said, stretching and pressing herself against him. He squeezed her gently.

"Should we get up and go face the music?" he asked.

The other boys will be occupied with food for quite some time and I'm ready to leave his bed. "Not yet," she replied. "Hold me a little longer."

"Okay," Josiah agreed easily, snuggling Annie close and kissing her forehead. She smiled, enjoying being cherished.

* * *

While Lucien and Sarahi had intended their wedding to be private, the previously unheard-of joining of Succubus and Naphil ended up drawing quite a crowd. One was Nathaniel, one of the youngest Nephilim. He'd been a newborn when the Flood occurred. No sooner had the announcement of Lucien and Sarahi's imminent nuptials been made than the golden-skinned man raced down the hall to a bedroom he'd passed many times, wishing he had the freedom to go inside. He knocked. A woman of about forty, with long hair the color of tea, answered the door.

Her eyes widened at the sight of Nathaniel. They nearly popped right out when he hauled her into his arms and kissed her. "Come on, Mary!" he urged, taking her hand and dragging her down the hallway towards the chapel.

"Nathaniel, what's happening?" the woman protested, tugging on his arm.

"Trust me. Things are changing. You have to see this to believe it."

They arrived a few steps behind Sarahi and slipped into a pew near the back. Mary looked up to the front of the chapel and her hand tightened in Nathanial's when she realized what was happening. Weddings at the compound were generally brief, and this one seemed to go faster than most. Within ten minutes the Naphil Lucien and the Succubus Sarahi were pronounced husband and wife.

As the happy couple tugged each other down the aisle, clearly intent on finding a bit of privacy in which to celebrate their union, Nathaniel whispered, "What about you, Mary?"

She looked at him, not understanding his question.

"They've revoked our vow of celibacy. The Nephilim are allowed to take wives. Will you be mine?"

She blinked. "I can't do that, Nathaniel," she said sadly.

"Why?" he asked, feeling as though his heart were about to break. "You know how long I've loved you."

"I know, but, Nathaniel, I'm already middle-aged. We would have so few years together, and I already look old. It would be ridiculous."

"I'm much older than you," he said, puzzled by her reaction.

"I know, but you're ageless."

"Mary, I don't care about that. I would rather have you for whatever time is allotted to us than miss out altogether. I love you. Don't you love me, Mary?"

"Of course, I do," she agreed.

"Good, come on." He led her to the front of the room, where the rather shell-shocked looking elder still stood.

"Mr. Smith," Nathaniel said, "do you have time for one more wedding?"

The elder looked at the two of them, opened his mouth as though to speak, and then closed it again, instead replying to their request with a brief nod.

Chapter 16

In the morning, Sarahi and Lucien wandered, hand in hand down the hallway to the dining room. Adjoining the kitchen, the massive space doubled as a meeting hall and auditorium. Every surface from the cinder block walls to the laminate floor, even the tile ceiling gleamed in shiny white. A row of narrow windows near that ceiling admitted pale winter sun.

Milling clerics, Nephilim, and children filled the room, just like any other day, apart from an excited buzz that hummed just below the surface.

Mr. Smith stared blearily into a cup of coffee as the newlyweds slipped onto the bench across the table. Lucien set down a tray laden with a huge breakfast. Sarahi carried a glass of juice and a muffin. Mr. Smith glanced up from his drink and eyed the Succubus.

"I didn't think you needed that," he said, indicating the food.

"I don't need it," she replied. "But I can eat if I want to. It's easier for people if I do now and again. Helps them forget." She smiled and laid her head on Lucien's shoulder. He squeezed her gently and then tucked into his food without a word.

"Mr. Smith," Sarahi said hesitantly, "could I ask a favor of you?"

He raised one eyebrow.

"There are a few of my sisters whom I believe... well, I think they would leave Mother if we offered them sanctuary here."

The second eyebrow joined the first. "I'm not sure inviting Succubi into the compound is a good idea. How do you know you can trust them?"

"They're my sisters," she said.

"And how would they be fed?"

"The same way I was. There's enough love energy in this place right now to feed a dozen Succubi."

"A dozen?" He slapped both hands on the table and leaned forward.

She shook her head, suppressing a laugh. "No. There are not twelve who are trustworthy."

"How many then?" he asked.

"Three for sure. At most five."

Smith inhaled deeply and then released his breath in a resigned sigh. "I suppose you can invite them. But I'm still not sure how you can be so certain they won't turn on us."

"I'll check them out," Lucien said between bites of ham and mushroom omelet. "I can tell by their auras if they're trustworthy."

"Oh, all right then," Mr. Smith rolled his eyes toward heaven. "I guess having a few more with inside knowledge won't hurt. But you'd better be certain they understand that they have to leave their sluttish ways behind them. I won't have that here."

Sarahi nodded. *Explaining to my sisters that they will have to feed by standing nearby while others make love is going to be interesting.*

A tall figure slid into the seat beside them.

"Good morning, Annie," Sarahi said warmly.

"Good morning." The girl blushed, lowering her gaze to her cup of tea. Luckily, Mr. Smith was examining his coffee again as though it contained the answers to all the perplexing questions that had arisen of late.

Sarahi poked the girl in the ribs and wrinkled her nose. Annie grinned through her blush. It had only taken the tiniest push to break through her restraint. And Annie, though embarrassed, clearly had no regrets. *Thank Heaven.*

"I've been wondering something," Sarahi said, making idle conversation.

"What's that?" Annie asked, her eyes begging for discretion.

"How is it that the Nephilim and the clerics came to work together? And how did the clerics gain the power to make rules for semi-angelic beings?"

"Oh, I know the answer to that," Annie replied. "After the Flood, there were thousands of Nephilim, but over the centuries, many were lost. By the Middle Ages, they were down to about six hundred. It was decided there were not enough left to police the whole known world, and so they began to gather the gifted from among the human race and train them to fight Succubi. Eventually, the Order of Clerics emerged, similar to Knights Templar, but much more secretive. They have declined greatly in ability, but at their height, around the time of the Renaissance, the clerics had great gifts; healing, prophecy, supernatural speed, strength and endurance. Most of those eventually dwindled or died out."

"That's amazing," Sarahi said. "How do you know all that?"

"The same way you know so much about the Incubus. I studied. I teach, so I have to know things."

"Why were the gifts lost?"

"We don't exactly know. Perhaps too many mundanes were brought in to prevent inbreeding and the bloodline thinned out. For the longest time, clerics were nothing but soldiers. That is, until recently."

"What do you mean?" Lucien leaned forward so he could see Annie as he asked the question.

"Well, grandfather is a prophet."

Mr. Smith met his granddaughter's eyes. She challenged him with a glare, and he nodded in agreement. "It's true. I do see visions from time to time."

"And when he sees one, it's guaranteed to be true," Annie added. "And there are others who have abilities."

"What others?" Mr. Smith asked her sharply.

The girl's expression turned mischievous. She stood and passed behind Sarahi, stopping by Lucien. "Allow me to demonstrate. Sir, do you trust me?"

"Yes, Annie," he replied. "What are you going to do?"

"You'll see." The girl closed her eyes and concentrated. A pure white light shone around her, eventually drawing down along her body to her hand, and then reaching the tip of her index finger. "May I touch you?" she asked.

Lucien nodded. Even though she hadn't opened her eyes, she seemed to know he had granted permission. She laid her fingertip against the scar on his face, tracing it along the length of the injury. Her finger followed the scar with unerring accuracy. When she had stroked the entire length, her hand dropped to her side and the light disappeared.

Sarahi looked at Lucien's face and gasped. The scar was gone as though it had never been.

"It seems I have a gift of healing," Annie said smugly as she returned to her breakfast. Josiah joined them, daring to slide silently onto the bench next to Annie. His whole body vibrated with tension, and Sarahi reached around Annie's back to touch his shoulder. When he glanced at Sarahi, she winked. He smiled, but it looked strained.

"Sir," Josiah said hesitantly to Mr. Smith.

Smith scowled. "I have nothing to say to you, Josiah. Get away from my granddaughter this minute. Go."

"No, sir," Josiah said. "I have something I need to tell you." He raised his chin, meeting the man's eyes.

Sarahi looked from her son to the elder. *This is not going to be pretty.*

"Well, boy, say your piece and be done with it."

"Very well. I love Annie." He slipped his hand into hers. "She loves me. I want to be with her."

"No," Mr. Smith said.

Josiah narrowed his eyes. "You mistake me, sir. I wasn't asking permission. I want to be with her, and I will be. You can't stop it."

A vein in Mr. Smith's temple began to throb. His teeth ground together audibly. "What did I tell you, Josiah? What did I say would happen if you went near Annie again? Do you want to be thrown out?"

"No, sir," Josiah replied.

"Then get away from her, and me. *NOW*!" His voice rose to a roar. Conversations stopped around the room as people turned to stare.

"No, Grandfather," Annie said. "You can't do this. You've never been fair to Josiah. Why do you dislike him so much?"

"He's an unnatural creature, the bastard son of a Naphil and a..."

"Stop!" Sarahi exclaimed. "That's no way to tell him."

"Tell me what? Child of a what?"

"Succubus." Mr. Smith spat out the word as though it were an insect that had flown into his mouth.

Josiah went pale. "Mother?"

She gave a short nod. He gulped. Suddenly, the expression on his face became haunted. He looked from one person to another, begging for help.

"Do you understand, Josiah? Do you understand why I didn't want you for Annie? She deserves better than to be saddled with a demon."

"You watch yourself, Mr. Smith," Sarahi hissed. "Why accept me and not him? Have you been tormenting him his whole life?"

"He has," Annie said. "And that was long before we knew what you were, Sarahi. He has some kind of prejudice against Josiah."

"After what happened three years ago, how can you still defend him?" Smith groused.

Annie leveled a defiant glare on her grandfather and drawled, "What? When I almost gave him my virginity? I wish I had."

Oh dear. Here we go.

"He manipulated you," Smith insisted.

Annie's caramel-colored skin turned a violent red. She opened her mouth to blast the old man, but Josiah spoke first, in a hesitant, uncertain voice. "I may have." He turned to face Sarahi. "Mother, is it possible?"

Sarahi shook her head. "We cannot create desire where none exists," she explained. "We can only enhance what's already there. If you influenced Annie, it was only by acting on feelings she already had."

"That's right," Annie agreed, chin stuck out defiantly. "I wanted him. I didn't feel manipulated."

"I didn't know what I was doing." Josiah cast his eyes down at the table.

Annie slipped her arm around him. "I love you, Josiah." He leaned his head on her shoulder but did not respond.

These people with their secrets and misconceptions. Sarahi rolled her eyes upward. The idea that desire is a sin leaves human youths in an impossible bind, but for Josiah, celibacy must have been excruciating. "When a Succubus, or in your case an Incubus, comes into puberty, son," Sarahi explained, "that ability to enhance can flare without warning. Likely you got caught up in it yourself, not realizing what was happening."

He nodded, swallowing hard.

"But I thought the age of marriage here was twenty," Sarahi continued. "If anyone should have married young, it's Josiah. Why was he not given a wife?"

Mr. Smith paid no attention to the question. He glared at the young couple in front of him. "Get your hand off him, Annie."

She shook her head. "I won't. You will not take me away from him again."

"I will make him leave," Smith snarled.

"Mr. Smith," Sarahi gasped, "consider. If you throw him out, what will become of us? *She* will find him."

"Who?" Josiah turned to Sarahi, confusion twisting his features.

"My mother. Lilith."

"The demon queen is your mother? That's what I come from? I've been training all my life to kill Succubi, and now you tell me I am one?" He gagged.

"Most of them need killing," Sarahi replied darkly. "Especially Mother. Promise me, Josiah. Promise you won't go to her."

He shook his head, not hearing what she was saying. "I'm a demon?"

"No, son, you're not," Sarahi said, laying a hand on his arm. "Demon is a choice. You are the Incubus, but you're only a demon if you act like one. I've chosen a different path, and I've got more of that blood than you do. Please, Josiah, calm down. Mr. Smith, calm down. This is not helpful. The important thing is the fight that is coming. In order to succeed, we need everyone working together."

"I will not work together with that!" Mr. Smith snarled, stabbing a thick, gnarled finger at Josiah.

"You're not thinking clearly," Lucien said softly. "Your hatred of Josiah is causing you to make bad decisions. We need him if we want a chance to win."

"We need Annie, not that creature. I've seen it, and my visions are never wrong."

Annie snorted, rolling her eyes. "Well, Grandfather, at this point, wherever Josiah goes, I go. I am my beloved's and my beloved is mine. So, if you want me here, you have to make peace with Josiah, and with us being together. Now that I have him, I'm never letting him go." Her arm tightened around the lad, but the look he turned on her was pure panic.

The words from Song of Solomon registered on Mr. Smith with all their significance. His dark face took on a purplish hue and he seemed to be choking. "Tell me, Annie," he managed to force out, "that you didn't... that you haven't..."

Annie's cheeks turned red, but she didn't answer.

"This was your doing!" Mr. Smith turned the full force of his rage on Sarahi. "My granddaughter is a modest, quiet girl. You used your sluttish powers to influence her, didn't you? You wanted me to give Annie to your demon son, and when I refused, you took matters into your own hands!"

"It's true, isn't it, Mother?" Josiah asked softly. "When Annie came to me yesterday, she didn't seem like herself. Did you influence her?"

Oh dear. I'm in for it now.

"NO!" Annie insisted. "No one influenced me. I wanted Josiah and I couldn't stand to wait another minute."

"But why right then? Mother had left just a moment before you arrived, right? Why did you come in?"

Annie looked Josiah right in the eyes and lied. "I didn't see your mother. I just felt you were in there, and I wanted to see you, so I came in. Then, when I saw you, I had to have you."

Josiah shook his head. "Nice try, Annie. Mother, why is it so important for Annie to sleep with me? What was that about? You say I'm an Incubus. That's more than a male Succubus, isn't it? What is it about me you want to control?"

Sarahi shook her head. *This plan is rapidly falling to pieces.* "You're looking at it the wrong way," she said. "You should have been married to Annie years ago. You need that connection. You need to be loyal to the Nephilim, to the clerics. They need you too. I was just trying to help the process along. It's necessary..."

Josiah scowled. "So, you manipulated us both, and now there's no way Mr. Smith will ever give me a chance."

"To be honest, son," Lucien interjected, "he never would have anyway."

"That's for sure," the elder sneered.

"Well I'm certain about one thing," Josiah said. "Whatever it is you think I need to do, I will not be anyone's pawn. I make my own decisions." He rose stiffly from the table and stalked away.

Sarahi rose to go after him, but Lucien held her back. "Give him some space."

"Give me some space too," Mr. Smith said. "Lucien, take your... wife away."

Lucien nodded, wrapping his arm around Sarahi and walking her back to their bedroom. From the corner of her eye, she saw Annie sneaking down the hallway towards Josiah.

"Did I do wrong?" she asked Lucien.

"I don't know, love," Lucien admitted, his expression far from approving. "People object to being manipulated."

"But I only gave her the tiniest nudge," Sarahi protested to the only person who would listen.

Lucien frowned. "I know, and you're right. They should have been married a year ago. I've suggested it more than once."

"Why is everyone so afraid of Mr. Smith?" Sarahi demanded. "He's not the only elder, and this attitude doesn't bode well for his leadership skills."

"No one is afraid, exactly," Lucien replied. "Respectful is more like it. He has visions of the future, and they always come true. Between that and his natural charisma, he's a great leader."

"Not when he's putting his entire society in jeopardy because of squeamishness and bigotry," Sarahi pointed out darkly, her own ire rising.

"Be calm, love. The Succubi have been our enemies for millennia, since the dawn of time. Asking them to accept you was difficult, but asking them to accept the merging of our lines might be too much."

Sarahi sighed. "I don't understand why. Our son is less demon than I am. I know Mr. Smith doesn't trust me, but he doesn't hate me, so why does he hate Josiah?"

"I'm not sure." A look of deep concentration rolled across Lucien's face as he struggled to explain the bizarre behavior this otherwise powerful leader displayed toward their son. "Part of it is natural protectiveness. He's lost so many people he loved, including most of his family. Annie is the only family he has left."

"But, Lucien, he's an old man. His granddaughter will be alone forever if no one is good enough to approach her, and he won't be around forever to keep her company."

Lucien dipped his chin in acknowledgment but did not speak.

A man's irrational protectiveness of female descendants is something I've heard about. Some of the drones even display a slight paternal connection... if they survive long enough.

Lucien continued. "Part of it is that Josiah's existence made him question so much of what he's always believed about Nephilim. I think he was quite uncomfortable with the idea that we might not want the vows of celibacy, and that he might be responsible for denying us a basic need that humans take for granted. The fact that I wanted you more than I wanted to keep my vow was the first blow to his worldview. The fact that I was able to produce a child was the second. So long as no Nephilim fathered children, it was easier to pretend those needs didn't exist. My actions forced him to reconsider his own."

"But to take his discomfort out on a child..."

Lucien's forehead crinkled. "I doubt he saw it that way. More likely he just didn't want the corrupted bloodline in his family. Annie is much stronger than he gives her credit for."

"Yes, I know." Sarahi considered telling him that Annie was The Assassin but decided against it. *That is not my secret to disclose.*

They arrived at the bedroom and Lucien led Sarahi inside, shutting the door behind them.

* * *

"Josiah." Annie stepped into the dormitory and approached him cautiously. A few paces away, she ran the rest of the distance and threw her arms around his neck. He turned in her arms and kissed her briefly before wrenching himself out of her embrace.

"Josiah, what's wrong?" she demanded. "Grandfather was way out of line, but really, what does his opinion matter?"

"It matters," he said darkly.

"Why?"

"You belong here. I never have. I have to leave, Annie." He drew air unsteadily into his lungs.

"Leave?" She grasped his arm. "You can't leave. Where would you go? What about what your mother said?"

He narrowed his eyes. "I have a hard time trusting a mother I've known since yesterday. Everything she said this morning made it sound like they need to control me. If she truly is a Succubus, my mother or not, I don't trust her."

"I trust her," Annie said.

"Why?"

"I've known her for a couple of years," Annie explained. "She's been passing me information about the locations of the Succubi. Her intel has led to dozens of successful battles, and do you know how she got that information? She went to the hive, right into Lilith's presence. Do you know what Lilith would have done to her if she'd been caught? It wouldn't have been pretty. She risked her neck for us many times. I'm the one who brought her here. She's my friend."

"She manipulated you into my bed. I didn't want that, Annie." Humiliation flared in Josiah's eyes. Annie could watch him turning their passionate encounter into a politically charged mistake.

"Liar," she snapped. *That was nothing but the love between us, you fool. If your mother gave a push, it didn't matter. This was inevitable.*

"Okay, I wanted you. I still want you." He took her arms in his hands and skewered her with an intense, green-eyed gaze.

Thank goodness. "You can have me, Josiah. I want you too. We've always belonged together."

He shook his head. "I can't. You deserve better than to be the lover of a bastard demon."

"I already am, Josiah," she reminded him. "Do you hear me complaining?"

"Why are you so determined, Annie? Are you part of this plot to keep my supposed 'powers' under control?"

Annie slapped him. While he still stood blinking in surprise at the blow, she hissed, "Idiot. Don't you know better than that? I wanted you long before your mother arrived, before I knew you were an Incubus. I've always loved you. I still love you, asshole. Now stop talking nonsense."

He laid a hand on his reddening cheek but didn't back down. "Are you sure you want me? What if I'm putting out some kind of demonic lure?"

She lifted her hand again and he flinched. "I know my own mind, Josiah. Never doubt that."

"Okay, okay," he said. "Forget it. You know your own mind."

"That's better," she said. "Cool off. No one is out to get you... well except maybe my grandfather. But he doesn't get to decide what's best for us."

"No, that's right. We make our own decisions." He closed his eyes. "I love you, Annie."

She smiled.

He squeezed her arm. "Listen, love. I need a little... space. And some time to think. Okay?"

Annie nodded. She kissed Josiah again and slipped out of the room.

* * *

At dinner time, Josiah did not appear at the table. Concerned, Sarahi knocked on the dormitory door. No one answered. Back in the dining room, the other boys reported they hadn't seen him since after breakfast. A thorough search of the compound revealed the devastating truth. Josiah was gone.

Chapter 17

Josiah had been missing for two weeks. Search parties had been sent in every direction, to no avail. It seemed as though he had vanished from the earth. Annie, of course, was devastated. So was Sarahi. The Succubus was wracked with guilt, convinced her interference that driven him away, and certain his desertion would spell certain doom for the clerics and the Nephilim.

They had requested reinforcements from Europe and Africa but had been refused. Both continents were rife with Succubi and could not spare a single warrior. Australia sent a few, and so did Asia, but the added troops only swelled the number of total angelic warriors from two to three hundred Nephilim, with an equal number of trained clerics. At last count, there were over two thousand Succubi active in North America. If they attacked the compound in force, along with the drones, the Nephilim stood little chance of success. If Lilith decided to join her daughters, there was no hope.

Each night, as she lay cradled in Lucien's arms, Sarahi reached out to her son, whispering to him, telling him how much she loved him and urging him to come home, but to no avail. He did not respond. The best that could be said was that he didn't push her away.

A week after that, four women approached the outer gate of the compound. Lucien emerged to meet them, his bride in tow. He'd just returned from another fruitless search and was eager to do something constructive.

"Sarahi!" The girls squealed, embracing her.

"Jael! Salome! Rahab! Sheba! And who is this?" Sarahi leaned over Salome to see the baby her sister was holding. "Another Succubus?"

Salome nodded, long black hair dancing around her dusky-skinned body. In deference to the cold, she'd dressed, for once. "Mother told me to expose her, to leave her outside to die, but... I couldn't."

"Why would she do that?" Lucien asked. "Why not have another soldier in her army?"

"She says she doesn't have time to care for a baby right now or a sister to devote to her upbringing. There's too much at stake. And... she said there was something wrong with the baby. It reminded her of...you." She turned to Sarahi. "She didn't want to risk it. But... a baby... you understand?"

"I do," Sarahi said. "She's our sister after all. Did Ruth not come?"

"Ruth's dead," Rahab said, casting her tilted green eyes to the ground. "She made Mother angry and..."

"How did she do that?" Sarahi asked.

"Her drone was a little... livelier than Mother wanted. He refused her."

Sarahi made a sympathetic face.

"Well, he was the lucky one," Sheba said dryly. She tore his throat out. He was dead in seconds. Poor Ruth." She shuddered.

Sarahi shook her head. *I do not want to think about it.*

"So, these are the sisters you trust?" Lucien asked, approaching the women. Sheba hissed and took several steps backward. Jael ducked behind a tree, her golden hair glinting in the sunshine. Salome turned, shielding the infant with her body. Rahab pulled two daggers from her belt.

"Sisters, please," Sarahi urged, "there's no need for this."

"But that's a Naphil," Salome whined.

"Yes. He's also my husband." Sarahi ran a hand along Lucien's thick bicep and took his hand, lacing their fingers together.

"Husband?" The daggers fell from Rahab's hands.

"Yes." Sarahi giggled. "Lucien, darling, these are my sisters Rahab, Salome, Jael, and Sheba. And... Salome, what's the baby's name?"

"She doesn't have one," Salome replied. "Mother couldn't be bothered. I couldn't just leave her there. Can she stay here too?"

"Of course," Sarahi said. "They won't turn away an innocent baby, will they Lucien? After all, they accepted Josiah."

Lucien nodded. "The child is fine. But ladies, we cannot simply admit you until we know you can be trusted. If… your mother knew we were here, it would be very bad for us."

"If Mother knew we were here, it would be worse for us," Salome said. "How can you know if we are trustworthy?"

"I can read your auras. Ladies, if you step forward, one by one, I will be able to see if you are able to enter."

"And if we're not?" Rahab asked. "Will you kill us? After all, we know where you live now."

"I cannot in good conscience harm a guest. If you are not safe to admit, I will remove you from this place, and you will not remember how to get back."

"Fair enough," the Succubus said. "Might as well start with me. What's my color, angel?"

Lucien squinted at the woman. "Red. Very bright. Contentious, but not necessarily evil. You have quite a gray overlay, but I'm not surprised you're feeling uncertain. Do you swear you will not go out of your way to cause trouble? Lilith will come, and when she does, our only chance is to prevent a united front."

"Yes," Rahab said. "That's true."

"So, you won't have the men fight over you?" Sarahi asked, raising an eyebrow.

"Not right now," Rahab replied with a hint of a smirk.

Lucien bowed his head to her, and she walked past him and through the open door. Jael stepped forward next.

"Green, though somewhat muddy."

"What do you mean?" The brown-haired Succubus asked.

"Nothing bad. Just that you might be feeling a little… sensitive…"

"Yes, darling," Sarahi interrupted. "Jael is very sensitive, but she doesn't like to talk about it. She also saved my life once. Let her in."

Lucien gave his wife a long look and then indicated the doorway.

"Sheba?" The blond Succubus approached.

Lucien recoiled, and in a flash, Sheba disappeared.

"Darling?"

Lucien rubbed his eyes as though he'd seen something painful. "That was the ugliest black aura I've ever seen. Sorry, darling. Sheba was a spy."

"Is she..."

"Sleeping in your trailer. When she wakes up, she will have no recollection of this meeting."

"Sir..." Salome stepped forward and held out the baby. "Please take her. Even if I'm not... worthy, I want to be sure this little one is safe."

Lucien smiled. "Bring her in yourself, sister. I've never seen such a beautiful blue aura, even on a full-blooded human. You are welcome here."

Tears glittered in Salome's eyes and she rose on tiptoe to kiss Lucien's cheek.

"If I may make a suggestion," he said, "I think this baby should be called Eve."

Salome nodded and walked through the door into the compound.

* * *

Josiah roared down the road on a second-hand motorcycle he'd taken in lieu of payment after helping out on a feedlot back in Nebraska. *How many states ago was that? I can't remember. A motorcycle is a cold way to travel in winter, and it doesn't hold much in the way of possessions, but I like it. And unlike a car or pickup, I have a license for this one.* It had been one of the things he and Father had done together when he was a teen.

Father. Sometimes I miss him. Sometimes not. Lucien could be interesting, but he was still stuffy, pompous, and inclined to talk rather than listen. Those were all deadly flaws to a twenty-one-year-old would-be rebel. *It's easy to stay away from Father. Mom's harder. No matter that I've only known her one day, the sparkling, rose-colored image has been part of me as long as I can remember.* She still came to him, singing, hugging him, and begging him to come home. Telling him how much she loved him. *Love, ha. Love doesn't manipulate. And what kind of mother arranges for her son to have a tryst with a girl?* A demon mothers. *I don't want to see her either.*

Annie. Josiah wanted to close his eyes but riding a motorcycle at speeds in excess of sixty miles an hour without looking where you where you were going was a good way to become a splatter against the side of that oak tree over there. *Sweet Annie. I miss her.* He dreamed of her nearly as often as he dreamed of his mother, but Annie couldn't caress his mind the way a demon could. *I believe her that she wasn't in on the plan to control me. We've known each other too long, loved each other too long, for me to think otherwise.*

Back before you knew you were a demon.

This time he did close his eyes. Just a quick blink to prevent the sting from becoming tears. *Annie is so powerfully good. I've seen her shining white aura. She's more angel than I am, despite having only human DNA. She deserves a human husband. Or maybe a Naphil, since they were allowed to marry now.* He could see that being a good match.

Actually, he *could* see it in his mind's eye. Annie would forget about him in the wake of a half-angel's love. *Surely if Father could love and even marry a Succubus, a creature who'd no doubt had hundreds of partners in her lifetime, another Naphil could forgive Annie her one indiscretion. Or rather her one afternoon of indiscretions.* Even as his teeth ground at the thought of her marrying someone else, he couldn't help but take a bit of satisfaction in knowing he'd been first.

Josiah's stomach growled. He'd been riding since dawn, hardly stopping to stretch his legs, and the sun hung low in the sky. He needed to eat. He pulled his bike into a sleazy-looking truck stop off the interstate and walked inside. The smell of greasy burgers and bad coffee nearly choked him, but a quick glance at the white plastic menu above the counter convinced him this was the place. *I need to pick up work again soon or I won't be able to afford more gas for the bike.*

"Burger and a beer," he told the long-bearded man behind the counter.

"Wanna show me some ID, son?" the man said.

Josiah pulled out his license, demonstrating he was over 21, and the requested beverage quickly appeared. He took a swig. Then another. The alcohol hit him pretty fast, since he wasn't used to it and his stomach was so empty. By the time the burger landed on the counter in front of him, he was too dizzy to stand up. Hoping the greasy meal would help sop up some of the excess, he tucked in, barely noticing when a person slid onto the bar stool beside him. That is, until a sultry female voice spoke. "Howdy, handsome."

He turned and looked into familiar lamp-like eyes in a pale, pretty face, surrounded by a nimbus of curly brown hair. He gulped. *She reminds me of Annie.*

When she saw him, her eyes widened. "What are you?" the Succubus whispered.

"Same thing as you, I guess," he replied.

"Come with me," she urged, taking his hand and tugging him away from the bar to a private booth. He stumbled a bit but managed to make the walk.

She sat beside him, placed an arm around his shoulder and whispered in his ear, "There's no such thing as a male Succubus, so what the hell are you?"

"According to my mother, I'm an Incubus."

She took his chin in her hand and turned him to face her. "Incubus?"

He nodded. *I probably shouldn't have said that,* he realized, a moment too late.

"My mother would love to meet you!" the girl enthused.

Josiah considered her suggestion. I *make my own decisions. Can't make good ones without the relevant information. I need to know what I'm up against.* "Take me to her."

* * *

Two weeks later, most of the Nephilim and all three remaining Succubi were married. Jael had scooped up Jonas the first night after their arrival. A week later Rahab said her vows with Peter. Sarahi had managed to convince the elders the boy would not turn as long as the

Succubus did not feed exclusively on him, and certainly enough love energy floated around to fill in the gaps. Finally, Nathaniel's older brother wooed and won Salome. Having the bad girls securely attached to husbands made everyone feel much better about their presence. They also proved invaluable in surprising areas. Salome possessed a gift for caring for children. Once the mothers became accustomed to her, they were grateful for the opportunity to get a little break now and again. Jael turned out to be a marvelous educator. She taught the Council of Elders things about the Succubi they had never imagined. And fiery Rahab had a firm grasp of the strengths and weaknesses of the Succubi and drones, and even a few tidbits about Lilith herself, which she was quick to share with the generals.

Despite these small gains, they could find no sign of Josiah. Sarahi began to despair of ever finding her son and refused to be comforted. Her darkest moment came one night when she reached out to his spirit, and he shut her out, like a door slamming in her face.

Sarahi came fully awake with a gasp, tears pouring down her face.

"What's wrong, love?" Lucien asked.

"She has him," she whispered. "He's gone to her." She drew her knees up to her chest and rocked.

Part IV

Chapter 18

Josiah stretched, sitting up in the bed. His nose wrinkled. *I will never grow accustomed to the stink in this place; a combination of snake, old sex, and blood. And it's cold. Always cold. Always dark.* Though he'd learned to capture light using the demon eyes he'd inherited from his mother, the dim fire didn't give him much to work with. *Maybe that's better. I really don't want to see what surrounds me.*

Beside him, a girl sat up and he slipped his arm around her shoulders. *Succubi aren't so bad, not really. This one seems young and pretty. She reminds me of Annie, except for the eyes and forked tongue.* She wanted him too, they all did, but for some reason, he didn't want her. *Maybe because she's so much like Annie.* But he was willing to cuddle up with her at night, just to keep warm, even though he had to wrestle to keep her wandering hands off him.

Josiah sighed. *This is not a nice place. I don't belong here either.* He'd thought, after spending his childhood rejected at the compound, maybe his demon relatives would be easier to fit in with. They weren't.

For one thing, they were all girls. There were men around, but Lilith kept them pretty busy. *Drones, they call them, and they seemed sort of... hypnotized. Or maybe like zombies. They appear to have no personality or will.* One walked past him in answer to the demon queen's call. The tall youth with shining mahogany hair had a vacant expression and moved like a sleepwalker. They all looked like that. The boy approached the demoness and she beckoned him closer, turning around to bend over her throne, wiggling her backside seductively. Josiah turned away. The first time he'd seen this spectacle, he'd been shocked and disgusted. Lilith's attempt to seduce him with blatant sex had not been successful. Too well he remembered having Annie in his arms. The hedonistic lifestyle of the hive paled in comparison.

Enraged by his prudishness, Lilith had backhanded him into the corner. *Damn, she's strong,* he recalled, rubbing the bruise on his jaw. *It would take a tank to stop her, or a charging rhinoceros.* The next night she'd come after him directly, using her unholy powers to enhance the lust he couldn't control when faced with her naked beauty. Josiah shuddered, at the memory, not only of his terrible mistake, but of the beating she'd inflicted on him afterward. He still couldn't figure out how she'd known he wasn't a virgin, but apparently it meant something to her. At any rate, he'd been positive she was going to kill him, until one of the girls whispered something in her ear. Just like that, she'd calmed down, stalking to her throne and flinging herself onto it, leaving him to nurse his injuries in silence.

A week later, she'd begun training him. The exercises resembled what he'd done at the compound, only much more vigorous. Now, after a few weeks, he'd laid a layer of muscle over his wiry frame. *At least the bulk makes me look more like a man instead of a skinny string bean of a boy.* And there were other... compensations. Any girl he wanted, any time. *Not that I want any of them, but they're not bad to look at.* Good food and plenty of alcohol lay around the hive, readily available, and there were live sex shows all over the place. It was a wild young man's paradise.

I want to go home. Only trouble was, he no longer knew where home would be.

It's not a place and you know it. It's a person. Anywhere is home, if Annie is there.

But Annie is not my future, he argued with himself. *I can't keep her. Is this really all that's left to me? This meaningless existence?* Josiah shook his head, tossed off the demon-girl's groping hands, and rose from the bed, pulling on a pair of ragged black trousers.

A loud crash shook Josiah the rest of the way awake. He turned to see the drone sprawled across the altar where the Succubi laid offerings of food and drink. *Apparently, Lilith's done with him. Poor fellow.* The demoness was like a mantis or a widow spider. The men who mated with her didn't always emerge alive.

That's another reason I'm not in a hurry for a repeat performance. Josiah shuddered again, averting his eyes from the pitiful, throatless corpse bleeding over the fresh bread he'd hoped to eat for breakfast.

Oh well. I'm not hungry now anyway.

"Josiah," the demon queen cooed in a sultry voice. He approached cautiously.

* * *

"We can't wait any longer," Jonas said irritably, slamming his hand down on the table of the council room. "If our enemy has the Incubus, we need to make preparations now."

"But how can we move forward without leadership?" Nathaniel asked, his arm wrapped around Mary's shoulders. The difference three weeks of marriage had wrought in her was astonishing. She looked ten years younger. It seemed some of her husband's vitality had rubbed off on his wife.

"Who says we're without leadership?" Rahab demanded. "Just because your pitiful elder has taken to his bed doesn't mean we're adrift. There's no reason why a human should be in charge anyway."

"Hey," Peter protested, poking his wife in the ribs. She nailed him with a furious glare, and he fell silent.

"I say Lucien should be in charge," Jonas proposed. "He's already General of all the Nephilim in North America. We follow his orders. We can't wait for Mr. Smith to decide whether he feels like doing his job."

"I agree," Nathaniel seconded, setting off murmurs of assent all around the table as clerics and Nephilim alike placed their trust in the tall half-angel.

Lucien inclined his head, accepting the appointment. "Very well. Let's be sure we understand what's happening. Sarahi, you've said from the beginning that if Lilith could secure Josiah, she would come after us. Why would she want to? Why start a war?"

Sarahi took a deep breath, contemplating her answer, but Jael jumped in first. "She might not. She might wait a few centuries hoping to kill off more Nephilim in skirmishes so that the takeover will be simple."

"But we all agree her goal is domination. It always has been. She will come against this compound first," Rahab added darkly.

"Why?" asked Mary. "There's an order of clerics on every inhabited continent. Why this particular one?"

"Because it's personal for her," Sarahi replied. "This is the compound where her traitor daughters are hiding. Where I am hiding. I defied her orders. I produced the child she wanted, and I did not give him to her. I orchestrated a plan to ensure that child would be unable to share power with her."

There were gulps and shudders around the table. The psychic scream that had rent the night a week ago had been horrifying, no less so because human and Naphil alike could hear it. Everyone knew what it meant. Lilith had discovered her prize had already imprinted on someone else.

"I don't think she'll wait," Salome said. "She's been growing angrier and more unstable for decades. And Sarahi is right, it is personal, but it's not Sarahi she wants to devour most.

Faces turned towards Annie, who was dressed in her Assassin uniform, but had left her face uncovered. She paled at the mention of that terrible moment, but then swallowed and straightened her stance. "Who would have guessed falling in love would be so hazardous," she quipped with a wan smile.

"Even if Lilith succeeded in wiping all Nephilim from the planet, the host of Heaven would be in no way depleted. Real angels cannot be killed, and the Creator will not allow Succubi to overrun His creation," Lucien said, shaking his head.

"Love, we're not dealing with a rational mind," Sarahi reminded her husband. "Lilith's hubris is beyond anything you can understand. She truly thinks she can challenge Heaven and win. Getting us out of the way is a step toward that end."

"So, our goal then is to protect ourselves and our families?" he asked. Sarahi nodded. "And how do we do that? Succubi, any suggestions?"

Jael, Sarahi, Rahab and Salome exchanged glances. "Don't waste time fighting drones more than is necessary. Stay away from the Succubi. If we can get rid of the source, the others will be leaderless. They can be scattered and dispersed much more easily. There is no second-in-command," Rahab said. The others nodded their agreement.

"Are you suggesting we concentrate the fight entirely on Lilith herself?" Jonas asked, appalled.

"Yes," his wife responded simply.

"Is that even possible with the Incubus's unlimited energy behind her?" Nathaniel asked. "I know she can't access it, but he can, right? If he fights for her, what happens?"

"I don't know," Sarahi replied. "But better to die trying than wait for the death she would dish out to us."

The ugly thought was far too true for anyone's comfort.

"So, what do we do then?" Jonas demanded. "If we want this fight on our terms, how do we draw her out? How do we make sure she doesn't just wait until our numbers are down? There are no new Nephilim. There will be no more. Every one we lose cannot be replaced. We will never be stronger than right now."

"I have an idea," Jael said.

"Tell us," Lucien urged.

The war council leaned forward. It was sure to be a desperate plan, but they had nothing else.

* * *

"Well, Jezebel," Lilith said irritably as she watched Josiah practice sword fighting with one of the drones. "Why do I have to keep him alive?"

"Mother," the Succubus cooed in a placating voice that made Lilith want to hit her, "For centuries you've dreamed of an Incubus. Now you have him. Why do you want him dead at this point?"

"The little prick gave away his power," Lilith snarled. "He slept with some girl and imprinted on her. All that lovely energy, and I can't drink a drop."

"He is tasty," Jezebel agreed, her eyes following Josiah's muscular back as he pressed his attack against the tall warrior.

This time, Lilith did hit her, sending her daughter sprawling. The woman rose quickly and returned without a word of complaint. Her pale cheek bore a palm-shaped red mark that would soon turn into a bruise.

"All right, Mother," Jezebel said. "All joking aside, it is possible to break the imprinting and rework it."

Lilith leaned over the arm of her chair until her face nearly touched Jezebel's. "How?"

"From what I've been reading, there is a provision for an unacceptable imprint. If the girl dies, it rebounds to his next partner."

Lilith nodded, considering the possibilities. "So, I have to...."

"Hunt down and destroy the girl who preceded you. But, Mother, you must also make him trust and desire you. Otherwise, he will not choose to give himself to you."

"Are you saying he does not desire me now?" Lilith hissed, rage bubbling at the suggestion.

"Please don't hit me again, Mother. I'm not trying to be insulting, but you have to admit he hasn't been too enthusiastic."

"What do you suggest?"

"Seducing a good-hearted man can be tricky. He's conflicted. I'd suggest you play up the problems he must have had with our enemies and show him how much better it is here."

Lilith nodded, pondering Jezebel's advice. *I've never before had to work at taking a man. They come to me, brainless and obedient. This will be an interesting challenge.*

Chapter 19

For the next three weeks, targeted attacks on Succubus strongholds increased in frequency and intensity. Clerics and Nephilim engaged in hit and run tactics, firebombing buildings, planting snipers to take out targets and generally doing anything they could to reduce the number of their enemies as drastically as possible. They made no attempt to cover their tracks. Soon Succubus intel knew the exact location of the compound and had a good approximation of how many Nephilim and clerics operated out of that location.

Examining the reports spread across the elders' conference table, Lucien considered their progress.

The information they had carefully fed to the enemy showed a stronghold in the Mojave Desert and a force approximately half of what actually existed. *When the stakes are this high, it's no time to play fair.* Lucien ruthlessly used every advantage available to him.

The risky decision had been made to avoid drawing Lilith to the actual compound. Its location remained concealed, so the young, old and vulnerable would be able to hide there. Finally, the Succubi had taught them how to enter the hive by opening a portal into the demonic realm where Lilith held court; a small world of eternal ice. All the Nephilim, and those clerics, like Annie, who had regained special gifts, were able to access it. *It's no different than relocating from one spot on earth to another, now that we know the coordinates. Who would have guessed it would be so easy?*

Then he recalled their plan and frowned. *We must be mad even to consider such an option, and yet, what choice do we have?* The intention was to open the portal and send in a few troops, who would appear in the demonic realm and attract the attention of the enemy. With luck, the majority of the Succubi would follow them back through the portal, leaving the queen lightly defended. Or better still, Lilith might come through herself. Either option would work. They had plans for both possibilities.

He scanned the coded document that held their plan. The date of the attack was set for December 31. With all the hype about the Y2K bug, anything strange appearing on computer screens and video feeds could be attributed to computer error.

That's tomorrow. Half-angel or no, Lucien's stomach churned with fear at the thought of what they faced. *It's like Sarahi suggested. Better to die fighting than to wait for Lilith to hunt us down.*

With a sigh, he gathered his notes and made his way to the cafeteria of the compound. There, Sarahi waited for him before the mass of clerics and Nephilim assembled for a final briefing.

"Does everyone understand what you need to do?" Lucien asked. There were nods all around. "Women and children will remain in the compound, along with the elders. We will maintain contact through the Succubi and any others with psychic abilities. This communication must only flow from the battle to the compound. Otherwise, you risk distracting your men while they are fighting."

Nods.

"Advance force," Lucien indicated a group of battle-scarred Nephilim and the youngest of the clerics, who sat apart from the body of the group. "Jonas will open a portal into the demon realm, and you will enter. Take no prisoners or hostages. Cut down as many as you can. Make noise and draw attention to yourselves, and then retreat. We want this to look like the skirmishes we've been enacting against nests on earth. The important thing is to leave the portal open. Remember, we need them to follow. And don't fight too skillfully. Make it look clumsy, so they won't suspect a trap."

The Nephilim saluted, fists to their hearts, as they had done since Roman times. The humans looked ready to piss themselves but imitated their angelic counterparts.

"First Battalion, set up at your coordinates in the Mojave Desert. When the Advance Team returns, send them through the ranks to the rendezvous point. Engage and hold any of the enemy who emerge through the portal. It is vital you hold the line."

Clerics young and old and ageless Nephilim all wore matching expressions of grim determination.

"Second Battalion, wait at the rendezvous point. Triage the Advance Force as needed and wait for the call for reinforcements. If Lilith emerges, engage her. If not, prepare to enter the hive through the second portal and engage her there. I will be with the Second Battalion."

The second group of men and angels dipped their heads in acknowledgment of their instructions. They had all been briefed and trained. They were all ready... *as ready as anyone could ever be in the face of certain death at the hand of a powerful, sadistic enemy.* Lucien concluded his speech. "I know this is asking a lot, but sleep, if you can. We cannot afford to enter this battle exhausted."

Incredulous stares met this advice. Adrenaline, not rest, would be the foundation of their strength.

"Now, let me turn the floor over to Sarahi. She has several suggestions for you."

Trembling with nerves, his wife stepped forward. "Here are some things you need to know. A Succubus is not much more than a strong woman with claws. They can be killed by a headshot, by having their throats or hearts removed, or by severing the spine. High caliber firearms should be effective, and I highly recommend taking out as many as you can before they get close enough to grab you. They're quite adept at hand-to-hand combat, but Lilith is tremendously old-fashioned. After the sword was invented, she didn't really acknowledge the development of other weapons. Shoot them if you can. A Succubus decomposes instantly, so if they don't go poof, they can still kill you." Her lame attempt at humor inspired a few tepid smiles. She continued. "Severing limbs slows them down but doesn't stop them. Apart from their claws, their greatest weapon is their allure."

"But, ma'am," Jonas protested, "they've never used that against us."

She raised an eyebrow at him. "That's because they didn't realize it would be effective. They, like the clerics, believed Nephilim to be asexual. Now that they know better, they will try it. Which brings me to my last piece of advice. Go back to your rooms with your wives and be sure that, come morning, the allure will have no power over you. Ladies, you have a responsibility to protect your husbands from the threat of dirty lust. No matter how tired, scared, or even sick you might feel tonight, there is no excuse for refusing. Protect your man with your love. You just might save his life." She looked at Lucien and then back at the crowd. "I have nothing further to say."

"I do," a raspy voice spoke from the doorway. Unkempt and unshaven, Mr. Smith staggered to the front of the room. "Let's pray." Hands folded. Heads bowed. Sarahi slipped her hand into Lucien's.

"Lord, we face the fight of a lifetime. The outcome is in Your hands, and we trust You. Help us face Your enemies with courage. Amen."

"And please protect Josiah," Lucien added.

"Amen," echoed other voices around the room, and the war council broke up.

As couples drifted back towards their quarters, a tall woman in a white uniform approached Sarahi and Lucien.

"Annie," the Naphil acknowledged her.

"Call me Assassin," she replied. "I'm no longer interested in being Annie."

"It's not a bad thing to be vulnerable sometimes," Sarahi cautioned her softly.

"It's done me no good," the girl said. "Lucien..."

"No," he replied, "you may not fight. You'd be walking right into her hands."

"I don't care," Annie replied, her face dark with depression. "What's left for me here? I might as well die doing something useful."

Lucien narrowed his eyes. "Then I definitely don't want you fighting. She'll know, you know."

Annie nodded.

"Know what?" Sarahi asked.

"That your demon son left her with more than just a broken heart," Mr. Smith intoned from beside them. "She's pregnant. It's no wonder she wants to die."

"I don't want to die," Annie snarled, making a dismissive gesture with one hand. "I want to help. We all know we're not coming back. This is it. I'd rather go down fighting than wait trapped in this compound like a rat. She'll come, and when she does, those who don't fight will go down harder than those who do. Especially me."

"I can't believe you still love that demon," Mr. Smith mocked.

"Grandfather, be quiet," Annie snapped. "If you had been nicer to Josiah, he would have wanted to stay with us. We would have him on our side in this fight. There was never anything wrong with him and you know it." She turned her back on him, focusing all her attention on Lucien. "I need to see him. To see if there's anything left of the Josiah I know. Maybe there's a part of him that still loves me."

"I'm sure there is," Sarahi told the girl gently. "But he's been with her for weeks. He won't be the same boy you knew. He's seen too much now."

Annie raised her chin. "And maybe the part of him that's still Josiah is sick of all he's seen. I don't know why or how, I just know I have to be at that fight. And I won't be a liability, Lucien. You know how good I am."

"I do know, Annie," Lucien replied. "You've saved my hide often enough. But I'm not thinking of you as a soldier. I'm thinking of you as a daughter. I don't want to see you hurt."

Annie blinked, and then threw her arms around the Naphil. He hugged her back. Sarahi joined them.

"I love you both," the girl whispered.

"I hate to admit it," Mr. Smith said dryly, unmoved by the touching scene, "but I've had the vision over and over since her childhood. There is a chance for us to win this battle, but Annie has to be there. I don't know how it will work, but her presence is the key to victory."

"And will you be there too, Moses?" Lucien asked.

Mr. Smith nodded. "I need to be. I may be too old to fight, but I'm not so old I want to hide in the tower while others do the fighting."

Lucien nodded. "You will both be there. Assassin, prepare yourself for battle. Moses..."

"I know what I need to do. Get out of here, you two. I'll be with the First Battalion in the morning."

The Naphil and the Succubus took their leave.

* * *

"Annie," her grandfather said, "can you forgive an old man for being stupid?"

Annie sighed, lowering her gaze to the floor. Then she lifted her head and met his eyes with a fierce expression. "If it were stupidity or ignorance, Grandfather, I could let it go. But it was prejudice. And don't say anything about demons. You hated Josiah long before we knew. You drove him away."

Her grandfather broke eye contact. Shame hunched his shoulders. "I did. Now, for tactical reasons, I wish I hadn't, but I still don't think he's the one for you, Annie."

"There has never been anyone else for me, Grandfather." She rested her hand on her flat belly. "I miss him."

Smith squeezed his eyes shut. "Can you forgive me, Annie?"

Her glare faded to sorrow. "I'm past holding on to hating you for your choices. You have to live with the consequences. The only thing left for me to do is move forward. Do you hate me now, too? Now that I carry the seed of his mixed blood?"

"I could never hate you, Annie. But why couldn't you have loved a normal boy?"

She laughed, and it sounded bitter and harsh. "There are no normal boys here, Grandfather. Haven't you noticed? We're a bunch of gun-toting, right-wing crazies. Josiah's no stranger than the rest."

Mr. Smith made as though to argue, then stopped. "I guess you're growing up, Annie," he said at last. "Hard for an old man like me to see. You're not ten years old with a skinned knee anymore."

"No. I'm twenty-one with a broken heart."

"For what it's worth," he said, "I am sorry for the role I played."

"I'm going to try and lure him back," she announced, showing no shame.

"No offense, Annie," her grandfather said cautiously, "but do you really think you can out-seduce the queen of the Succubi?"

"Easily," she replied. "That bitch doesn't love Josiah. She can't have him. He's mine and I *will* fight for him."

She tossed her milk chocolate curls over her shoulder and stalked away.

* * *

In the little bedroom, Lucien lay on his back on the bed, cradling a naked Sarahi against his shoulder. He stroked the side of her face, her neck and her arm. She kissed his bare chest.

"I don't want to take your energy, darling," she said.

"I have it to give," he replied. "I want you, Sarahi." He leaned up and kissed her forehead.

"Did I cause all this?" she asked.

"All what?"

"This battle. If I had left you alone, if I hadn't seduced you, the Nephilim could have remained in the business of keeping balance and protecting the innocent. There would have been no need to declare outright war."

Lucien shook his head. "No, love, you didn't seduce me. I wanted to be with you. I came to find you, remember? Can you honestly say you regret loving me?"

"Of course not," she told him quickly. "Your love is the brightest, most wonderful thing in my entire existence. But what right do I have to love?"

He sighed. *Accept my love, darling. You are no monster.* "The same right as anyone. You deserve to be loved, Sarahi. And look at the good you've done. Your actions allowed the Nephilim finally to take wives, something they've wanted for centuries. Can you feel the love in this place tonight? All my brothers are holding their women. We have always faced death, and many have fallen, but now, finally, we have something worth fighting for, worth dying for. That's because of you, darling, your courage and determination. You're the best of your kind, Sarahi, and I love you."

She smiled and scooted up to kiss him. He took her lips, rolling her beneath him to ravish her mouth with blazing kisses. She kissed him back in a frenzy of desire. He released her mouth and rose to his knees, rolling her over onto her belly. He lowered his mouth and pressed heated kisses up the length of her spine, nipping and lapping at her tender skin. His hands delved beneath her, cupping her full breasts, rolling the nipples between his fingers.

Sarahi moaned and rose to her knees, presenting herself to her husband. Lucien flexed his hips, rubbing his erection over the smooth curve of Sarahi's bottom. Her silky skin caressed him, and he made a little growling noise. Pulling back, he sat, taking a moment to admire her beauty. Her skin glowed like alabaster in the moonlight; her burgundy hair spilled forward onto the white sheets. He rested one hand on the full curve of her bottom, stroking the soft skin again. Her feminine folds glistened with moisture. The little nub of her clitoris stood proudly erect, begging to be touched. He leaned forward and kissed it, then touched his tongue to the straining morsel.

"Ohhhh!" Sarahi sighed at the sweet stimulation. Lucien liked the sound. *I love knowing my lady's pleasure is the result of my actions.* He licked her again, and then again, making love to her with his mouth. Sarahi squirmed and twisted, whimpering. He held her still with his hand on her hip.

"Oh, Lucien!" She arched her back and shuddered as deep pleasure washed over her. Her flesh throbbed under the caress of his mouth. He wanted to experience that shuddering, so he positioned himself behind her and pressed into her welcoming depths.

The stimulation of his entry set of another round of ecstatic spasms and Sarahi buried her face in the pillow and wailed.

"Lovely woman," he murmured, "my dearest love." And then he began to pound into her, making her take every inch of his aching steel. She felt so good around him he wanted to climax immediately... and yet he wanted to postpone it as well. To enjoy her as long as he could. *This position is exciting, but somehow... not enough.* He slipped from her body.

"Lucien?"

"Turn over, love. I want to see your face."

Sarahi rolled to her back and urged her husband down on top of her, twining her legs around his. Lucien arched his hips and speared deep inside her again, lowering his mouth to cover her in kisses. He thrust hard and then slowed down, nudging, slipping through her wet, heated passage. Sarahi stroked his back with gentle hands, urging him to continue. Her body tensed on the brink of another orgasm and he gave a sharp thrust, catapulting her into ecstasy. Words of love mingled with pleasured gasps as he rode his lady through one peak and into another until he could no longer hold off, and his own groans of pleasure blended with hers.

Lucien cuddled Sarahi close, listening as her breathing slowed, caught, changed to sobs. He made no attempt to shush her. *What we face warrants a few tears. What warrior would not go off to battle bathed in the love of his woman?* He kissed her and tasted the salt on her skin. As soon as he recovered, he would have her again, but for now, he just needed to hold her.

Chapter 20

As sunrise broke over the Mojave Desert, sparkling cheerfully on the silver exterior of a deteriorating travel trailer, a shimmer of heat rose from the sand and scrub. Being the last day of the year, even the desert was not hot enough for a mirage, and, sure enough, this proved to be an illusion. A second glance revealed a force of abnormally tall men, robed in white. They represented every race and color on earth, and yet seemed somehow not of earth, at least not entirely. A matching number of ordinary-looking men fanned out among them. Some were tough and battle-scarred, others young, fresh-faced and flushed with the excitement of their first battle, but each man showed terror in their shifting eyes and tense posture. At their head, on the steps of the trailer, sat a man with gleaming ebony skin, glittering obsidian eyes, and jutting cheekbones that looked like they had been sculpted with an artist's tool. His jaw set in stubborn lines, but his eyes scanned the horizon far away. A scent of perfume and woman hung around him, wafting from a handkerchief tucked in the holster that held his pistol. He pulled out the rose-colored square and lifted it to his nose. His lips seemed to form a word... *Sarahi...* and then he returned his prize to its spot and resumed his watch over the shimmering sand.

* * *

Josiah sat at the foot of Lilith's throne. The demoness ran her claws gently through his hair, caressing his scalp. *I have to admit; she's been much nicer lately. I know she wants me on her side—and in her bed—but I can't commit to it. For what reason, I'm not certain. She's beautiful, and when she isn't being terrifying, awfully sexy. Maybe the problem is how often she chooses to be terrifying. Still, if I'm going to live as a demon, I need to make peace with their behavior.*

The stroking claws flattened, and she ran her palm down the back of his neck and over his shoulder. He rested his head on her knee. *This isn't the woman I want, but she might be the only one I can have. Make peace with it, Josiah. Let it be. You're a demon. She's a demon. Consort to the demon queen isn't such a bad thing. His heart clenched in protest of the thought, and his stomach threatened to invert itself.*

What is that strange shimmer over on the side of the room? Josiah's eyes narrowed. It appeared to be a mirage, wavering like heat in the desert.

"Ah, good. The ladies are back from Vegas. I could use some new drones... that is, unless you'd like a turn?" Lilith ran her claws lightly down his back.

"Maybe," he said, considering the option and concealing his disgust. "Will you promise not to tear my throat out afterward?"

"Oh, you silly boy. I would never do that to you. Come here, Josiah." She drew him to her throne and urged him onto the seat beside her, leaning down to kiss him. He accepted the kiss, pondered it. *Not too bad. I could get used to this...*

A scream erupted in the chamber, followed by another. Metal rang as swords slipped from sheaths.

BANG! *Is that a gun?* Josiah pulled away from Lilith and turned. White-clad figures, seven in all, stood in a circle, back to back, guns trained on the room.

"Open fire," a familiar, low-pitched voice snarled, and the soldiers began shooting Succubi and drones. The demonesses extended their claws and fangs, circling the clerics, looking for an opening, but the guns kept them back. Several fell as the circle of clerics and Nephilim slowly rotated. The motion brought into view a small figure with a mask covering the lower half of the face. His gaze became ensnared by brown eyes that met his and then flinched away.

"Josiah."

He closed his eyes. That beautiful, familiar voice rang in his head. He glanced at Lilith, and then back at Annie and felt dirty. *How could*

I have traded that innocent sweetness for this evilly lascivious demon queen?

Because you had to. Because Annie doesn't deserve a demon for a lover.

The girl had stopped firing and stood as though frozen, staring at him. He looked back intently. The Magnum trembled in her strong, capable hands.

Come back! He could hear the words in his head as though she had spoken aloud. *Come back, Josiah. Come home.* He drew in a shaky breath.

"Assassin," barked a commanding voice, "this is no time to lose focus! Fire!"

Annie aimed her weapon at Lilith and squeezed the trigger. The big demoness dodged, and the bullet lodged itself in her throne, splintering the wood.

"Enough," the voice barked again. "Fall back."

A shimmer lit up the chamber again and the soldiers slipped through it, one by one. Those at the end of the line provided cover as their friends retreated.

"Watch this," a sibilant voice murmured in his ear. Lilith reached back and made a throwing motion with one hand. The cleric at the end of the row stopped dead. She closed her hand and he fell to the floor just as the last of his companions disappeared through the portal back to earth.

Josiah struggled to maintain his detachment. He had no way of knowing whether the captured cleric was Annie. They all looked alike in their uniforms. He trotted along at Lilith's heels.

"How did you do that?" he asked her.

"It's easy. You just make your energy into a net. Once it wraps around your victim, it locks up their electromagnetic field, as well as their muscles. Now let's see what we have here.

She reached out and sank her claws into the shoulders of the cleric, lifting him to his feet. Josiah reached out and dragged away the cloth, which covered the face of...

"Peter?" *Unbelievable.* Lilith had captured the bully who had made Josiah's life unbearable for as long as he could remember. A wave of hatred and rage welled in him as he looked into that face.

"What are you doing here?" Lilith asked the boy.

He struggled not to break down in the face of so intimidating an enemy. "I don't need to answer you."

Energy swirled in the room. Lilith was bringing all her seductive power to play, trying to break down Peter's restraint. Josiah predicted it would work and was stunned when it didn't.

"Let me go," Peter said, his voice trembling but his jaw firm. *Well, Peter never did lack courage.*

"Oh, no," Lilith replied, stroking him under the chin with one long black claw. "You're done, I'm afraid. But you get to decide how you leave this life. Tell us just what in the name of Lucifer you are doing here, and I'll kill you quickly. And believe me, young man, you don't want to know how I can kill you slowly."

Peter gulped, his tanned face draining of color.

"How dare you infiltrate my home?"

He inhaled sharply through his nose, considering his options. Then, with a final show of bravado, he answered. "The stalemate has gone on long enough. We are here to issue an invitation. A challenge. Forget the game of cat and mouse. Come out of your hole and fight face-to-face."

"Are the Nephilim and their cronies so eager for destruction then? Very well. I see you're telling the truth." Lilith made a throwing motion and Peter flew through the air to crash into the far wall of the cave. He dangled several feet above the floor though hung from a hook.

"Josiah," Lilith said in her seductive voice, "is this boy your friend?"

"No," he replied, unable to keep the snarl from his voice.

"Good. I want to teach you something useful. Gather up all that yummy energy of yours."

Energy? He glanced at her, his eyebrow quirked.

"You're bubbling with it, fool. Gather it up!"

He'd never examined himself closely before. *Now that she mentions it, I can see myself surrounded by a muddy gray light.* He glanced around the room. Every creature had a similar glow. Lilith's gleamed black, like her ineffectual fire, but other colors danced around the Succubi and drones, all muddied, shadowed with gray, but clearly visible.

He concentrated, making a closing motion with his hand, and the energy hovering around him obediently gathered into a ball.

"Good boy. Now, make it longer and thinner, like a blade."

Josiah wasn't sure how he knew what to do, but he did.

"Reach out with your blade. Touch his aura."

The moment Josiah's energy touched Peter's he felt the boy's emotions, tasted them on the tip of his tongue. *Terror. Good. As many times as he's made me feel like shit, Peter deserves it. He deserves anything he gets, the bastard.*

"Push deeper. Push inside his body."

Peter screamed. Josiah ran his energy over the internal organs. *Clenching bowels. Pounding heart. Gasping lungs. Wildly firing brain.* He touched everything.

"Now, just send a burst of energy along the line from you to him, and you'll take care of this one for good."

Josiah paused. Considered. Images swirled in his head. Peter knocking him down and laughing, placing a foot on his throat… claiming Annie. Eyes narrowed, he sent not a pulse but a blast of pure, raw rage down the psychic cord between his aura and his lifelong nemesis.

As one, Peter's organs exploded inside his body. The strength of the blast forced blood from the boy's mouth, nose, and the corners of his eyes, where it ran like tears down his face. Lilith released her energy and Peter's corpse collapsed to the floor, where it lay like a broken puppet.

Josiah stared.

"Well done," the demon said, "but a little fast. Next time start at the toes and work your way up. They suffer more that way."

Josiah swallowed.

"Now then, our enemies have issued a challenge. We do not let challenges go unanswered. They want a fight; we will bring them one. They want to die; we will help them with that goal. Come on, Josiah. Let's show them what it means to come up against a superior force."

Lilith stalked away. Josiah stumbled to a dark corner and vomited.

* * *

Rahab's scream echoed through the entire compound. From all corners, the women ran to her.

Salome and Sarahi got there first, wrapping their arms around their sister.

"What is it?" Sarahi asked. "What's wrong?"

"It's Peter. It's my husband. He's dead!" She burst into hysterical sobs.

Sarahi stroked her back and Salome ran gentle fingers through her hair, trying to soothe her.

"Is this what it will be like for all of us?" Jael asked darkly. "Will we all know when our men die?"

"I don't know," Sarahi answered. "Probably."

* * *

"Report, Jonas," Lucien barked. "What happened?"

"The first stage of the plan seems to have been successful," the Middle Eastern looking half-angel reported. "We got into the hive and took down several Succubi and drones."

"Any casualties?"

Jonas nodded. "Peter didn't make it back. Do we go after him?"

Lucien shook his head. "No point. There's no way anyone will be able to get to him. We can only hope he's already dead. Anything else?"

"No," Jonas paused, considering, and then added, "but I think you'd better talk to The Assassin. She seems a little...shaken up."

And Jonas still seems a little shaken up to learn The Assassin, who has provided backup to so many missions, is a girl. But no matter. Striding away from the trailer, Lucien found Annie sitting on the sand, staring off across the desert, her arms wrapped around her knees.

"Annie?" He laid a hand on her shoulder. She turned, her mask hanging loose against her chest, a look of distress on her face. "What's wrong?"

"I saw him."

Lucien's heart clenched. He never spoke of it, but the thought of his son with that demon monster was tearing him up too. "You knew he would be there."

"Yes, but I didn't expect to see him. He was with her, right beside her throne. Have we lost Josiah forever?"

"I don't know," Lucien replied. "I hope not." He let the words hang between them for a moment before returning to soldier mode. "You have to shake it off, Annie. If you let your feelings distract you, you're going to get yourself killed, and probably others around you. Come on. Where's the warrior I know?"

She glanced away.

"Listen, if you can't pull it together, you'll have to go. I can't have you here if you're not mentally present. Go back to the compound with the other girls."

She turned angry eyes on him. "You need me."

"Not like this, we don't. Go on, Annie. Go home." Lucien turned his back on her.

She shot to her feet and grabbed his arm. He turned to meet her eyes with a quizzical expression.

She fastened the mask back over her mouth and nose. "Who's Annie? I'm The Assassin."

"Good girl."

A voice sounded inside Lucien's head. "General, where are you?"

"At the rendezvous point," he replied telepathically.

"Get your angel ass down to the portal right away," Nathaniel urged. "Something big is coming through!"

* * *

Something big indeed. A towering naked woman with black hair hanging to her knees, glowing, pupilless green eyes, four-inch claws, and huge back-curving fangs stepped onto earth. Her aura, black as tar, seemed to suck up the daylight. Around her, a host of women, claws and fangs extended, hissed and shifted. Among and between them, hundreds of men, their expressions vacant, hefted swords and spears, ready to do battle.

Nathaniel took a deep breath and sent a quick thought to his wife back at the compound. "Ready," he said to the company of Nephilim and clerics. They shouldered high-powered rifles. "Remember, the more you take out before they reach us, the better. On my mark."

"Kill them all!" the tall figure hissed, her voice sibilant as it whistled between fangs and over a forked tongue. The Succubi and drones rushed forward.

"Fire!" Nathaniel shouted. As one, his battalion squeezed the triggers of their weapons, sending bullets smashing into the oncoming mass of enemies. Screams rang out across the desert sky.

* * *

Salome drew in an unsteady breath.

"What is it?" Sarahi asked. "Is your husband...?"

"He's fine. It's not him. It's... oh no! It's my drones."

"What about them?"

"They're calling me. All around them, their brothers are dying. They're fighting for her, and I'm not there. They want to know what to do."

"They're asking *you?* I thought they belonged to *her!*"

"So did I. Oh, Sarahi, I can't abandon them!" Salome wailed. "They didn't ask for this. I have to go to them! Rahab, Jael, can't you hear them?"

Jael nodded, her lips compressed and pale. "Mine are calling too."

Rahab wiped her eyes and agreed. "Can't you hear them, Sarahi?"

She shook her head. "I've never made a drone. I couldn't. It was unfair."

They all stared at her.

"Well," Salome said at last, "I can't leave them like that. I have to go to them."

"What?" Sarahi gasped. "You're going back to Mother?"

"Of course not," her sister replied. "I'm going to set them free. They shouldn't have to fight and die for her."

Salome crossed her arms over her chest and disappeared.

"She's right," Jael said, following suit. A moment later, Rahab vanished too. Startled, Sarahi decided to follow her sisters. *I have to know what's going on.*

* * *

As the remaining Succubi and drones approached the line, Lucien sent a telepathic message to his commanders. "Move forward. Focus on the leader."

He could feel the reluctance in their acknowledgment. I *can't blame them. The towering demoness is incredibly intimidating. She looks like beautiful death.* But the thought of what would happen to his Sarahi, his bride, if this creature rose to power overcame his nerves and propelled him forward. Pulling out the two thin blades from their crossed sheaths on his back, Lucien waded into the fray, dodging and slashing.

A naked woman, beautiful and seductive, slunk towards him, radiating lust. Lucien scowled and swung one sword, reducing her to a shower of golden dust. *My lady was right to urge intimacy last night. Bathed in Sarahi's love, the power of the Succubi has no effect on me.* A quick glance showed his fellow soldiers equally unmoved. Seeing their favorite strategy ineffective, the girls switched to claws and fangs. They were damned fast and strong, their lean bodies honed by millennia of training and skirmishes.

A drone with a broadsword that would have suited a medieval knight came at Lucien, swinging his blade with an overhand movement meant to cleave the Naphil's skull. Lucien sidestepped, and the sword sank deep into the earth. Lucien ended the poor fellow's miserable existence with a quick slash to the throat. The body fell to the earth with a heavy thud, raising a cloud of desert dust, and decomposed instantly. *Perhaps he really was a medieval knight.*

Lucien moved forward again. This time, a smaller, slightly-built man engaged him. He had an Asian cast to his features and moved like a cat, thrusting and jabbing with a light, maneuverable sword. Lucien met him parry for parry, holding his own, not pressing the attack, but giving no advantage. *If this man were not a soldier in the enemy's army, he would have been a pleasure to spar with, but this is war.* With a sigh of regret, Lucien dodged past the whirling blade and opened the warrior's belly, spilling his entrails into the sand. The man fell to the ground shrieking, until Lucien delivered a coup de grâce through his heart.

Movement in his peripheral vision caught his attention and Lucien turned. On the hillside, four slender figures stood silhouetted against the horizon. Three made beckoning motions with their fingers and a few dozen drones abandoned the battle and walked towards the rise.

Another Succubus darted into Lucien's space, claws slashing, and he rejoined the battle with a sigh.

* * *

Sarahi looked down from the rise over the scene of battle. Pride swelled her heart as she saw how the brave company of angels and men held their own against a much larger force of demons. She could see Lucien, the connection between them telling her the tall dark figure cutting a swath through the mêlée was hers. *Maybe I can use that connection to help him. I'm full to overflowing with the loving he gave me last night.* She sent some of the energy back to him, not in a distracting burst, but a thin stream. *In the heat of battle, he might not even notice.*

Beside her, her sisters reached out towards the scene before them and called, beckoning with their hands. All through the mass of soldiers, men lifted their heads and turned, heedless of the enemies they'd been engaging. They marched as one away from the battle and stood, shoulder to shoulder, in front of the women who'd created them.

"Well, Salome," Jael said, "they're here. How do you figure on releasing them?"

"Rather simply, I think. We made them by draining away their life force, their will. I don't know about you, but I have enough excess energy to launch a rocket. Watch this."

The black-haired Succubus closed her eyes. Sarahi gasped. A cord like a golden string lay across the desert sand connecting her to one of the men, a young blond. She sent a pulse of energy through the cord and back into the man. Awareness dawned in his blue eyes.

"I'm sorry for what I did to you," Salome said softly. She made a slashing motion with her hand and the bond between them severed, the cord shriveling and disappearing. "You do not need to fight. Go in peace. There's a town a few miles in that direction." She indicated the north, away from the battle.

Interestingly, as the connection between the two faded, the man seemed to age visibly. No longer a handsome youth, he suddenly appeared to be in his mid-thirties. He nodded to Salome and turned, walking slowly away.

"How did you know what to do?" Rahab asked.

"I'm not sure," Salome replied. "I never thought about trying it before. I always thought the drones belonged to Mother."

"Did you see how he aged?" Jael asked. Some of these men are centuries old. If we release them, they will die."

Rahab nodded. "But they are human, and that is their destiny. I think, at least for mine, they would prefer to die as men than live as slaves." She sniffled, visibly steeled herself, and pulsed. A dozen thin cords flared and then shriveled. A moment later, three men walked towards town. Sarahi felt a pang of sympathy for the others, lying in various states of decomposition on the sand, but the flare of gratitude in their eyes as they regained their souls helped... a little.

* * *

Lucien fought his way through a pocket of drones. He really did try to avoid killing them. Some were staggeringly bad soldiers, and all were acting on under the volition of others. He knocked them out and pushed them aside, always pressing forward, always trying to get to Lilith. *I should be tired by now, but I'm still bubbling with fresh energy.*

Another warrior rose up between him and his target. Lucien ground his teeth in frustration. Long blond hair straggled down a powerful back. Blue eyes glittered with bloodlust. *This one isn't fully engulfed in the will of the Succubi. He fights at least in part because he wants to.* Lucien recognized the furry loincloth and heavy weapons of a Viking Berserker. The man was splattered from head to foot with blood and other, less mentionable things. He swung hard at Lucien, who dodged the blow and aimed low with his own sword, trying to take out the fellow's knees. The Viking jumped over the thrust and shot out a meaty fist, catching Lucien under the jaw and sending him sprawling in the dust. The battle ax fell, and Lucien scrambled back to avoid it, placing his hand squarely on something soft and wet. He risked a glance and regretted it. His hand had landed in the split-open chest of a dead cleric. The boy's intestines tangled around his fingers and he shook them loose. His moment of distraction came at a heavy price. With a wild yell, the Viking pounced, ready to land on Lucien with all his massive weight. Lucien braced for the blow, but serious injury was unavoidable. He closed his eyes.

A blast startled him back to awareness. The Viking lay sprawled on his back several feet away. The Assassin stood over Lucien, a shotgun braced against her shoulder, a wisp of smoke rising from the muzzle.

"You need to be more careful." Annie's amused voice came from behind the mask. "It's dangerous out here." She dropped the weapon and extended a hand, helping him to his feet.

"I didn't call for you, Assassin," he teased.

"I know," she replied. "You didn't have to. Now come on. There's an evil bitch over there who could use a bit of humbling."

Lucien nodded, reclaiming his sword from where it had fallen. Together they stalked into the fray once more.

* * *

"You know something?" Jael said from their perch above the battle. "Our men are doing better than I expected. They really are holding their own."

"They are," Sarahi agreed, "but Mother isn't fighting. She's just standing by. They'll be hard-pressed to take her after fighting through that lot."

"And she stands there," Rahab added darkly, "like the overgrown leech she is, letting her own daughters die so she can have an easier time of it."

"Is there anything else we can do?" Salome wanted to know.

Jael thought for a moment. "We could call our sisters. See if any of them are willing to walk away. Even a few could make a difference, especially if they take their drones with them."

"Good idea," Salome said. Joining hands, the four concentrated on calling their sisters, touching each heart with a summons.

* * *

Lucien blinked in surprise. Whereas the path before him had previously been clogged with fighters, suddenly large empty patches had opened up. With careful maneuvering, he and The Assassin wended their way through until they stood on empty ground, with nothing between them and the oversized form of their enemy. The enemy and her much smaller companion.

Lucien closed his eyes against a wave of pain. His son stood to one side and slightly behind Lilith.

"Josiah," Annie breathed beside him.

He nodded. "We can't worry about him now. We have a job to do."

"I know," Annie said, but her voice sounded unsteady.

"Don't go girly on me now, Assassin. Put Annie away a little longer." Then he called to Josiah, "Son, you don't have to do this. She has no power over you. You can leave at any time. Walk away."

"Son?" The demon laughed in her hissing, snake-like voice. "So, you're the one? Ah yes, you do look like my little darling." She turned and ran one long black claw down the center of Josiah's cheek. The boy did not react in any way.

"You know something," Lucien said, feigning bravado, "You are, without a doubt, the worst mother-in-law the world has ever known. Fortunately for me, my wife will not be angry if I kill you."

Lilith raised an eyebrow. "Wife?" She shook her head. "What a pathetic Succubus that Sarahi is. I should have eaten her when she was a baby. All right, angel, you want to fight? Have at me."

She stepped forward and her claws grew longer and longer until they became ten swords in the sunlight, black like the tarry darkness of her aura. Lucien drew his own blades. The two warriors regarded each other in silence, each weighing the threat. Then Lilith shot forward like a striking cobra, her claws flying straight towards Lucien's heart.

* * *

"What do you traitors want?" Cali demanded. "Why are you calling us away from the battle?"

"Why did you come?" Rahab retorted, answering the question with a question. "Jezebel isn't here. Neither is Herodias. Those truly loyal to Mother ignored us. You came. Why?"

"Maybe we're just curious," Cali snarled. "Why aren't you fighting?"

"Our husbands don't want us to," Sarahi replied. "They don't even know we're here."

"Husbands?" Cali asked, thunderstruck. "How can that work?"

"They're Nephilim. They're so deliciously strong," Jael cooed.

The sixteen Succubi on the hillside stared at their sisters.

"That sounds rather like sleeping with the enemy," Cali said.

"Well, it depends on your definition of enemy," Rahab replied, examining her fingernails with unwarranted intensity. "Mother sends you up against men and angels to protect her own hide. Our men are down there risking themselves to keep us safe. My husband..." She sobbed. "He died so I could be protected. Tell me which one sounds more like an enemy."

Cali acknowledged the truth of that with a curt nod. "And you too?" She turned to Sarahi, not quite believing that the lowest of the sisters would have secured such a prize.

"Oh, yes," Sarahi replied, looking over the battlefield. "Mine's the most magnificent one of them all. Just look." She indicated the area where Lilith stood. Before the demoness, Lucien's midnight skin gleamed with sweat in the desert sun. His muscles bulged as he held his swords at the ready. "My Lucien. Josiah's father. Isn't he glorious?"

"Are you saying we could have... all that?" Cali demanded, spurring a wave of murmurs from the other Succubi.

"Just imagine," Jael said. "A life without fear, without..." She waved her hand in Lilith's direction. "A husband who loves you. Even a child. It's all possible, sisters. But first, you need to step out of Lilith's realm. And take your drones with you. They're dying for you, not for her. They don't care about her, you know that. She'll just kill them anyway."

Cali considered. "So, what do you want us to do? Fight against her?"

"No," Salome said. "Just leave. Release your drones and go. Let the men save their strength to deal with her."

Cali looked out across the desert, considering the options.

* * *

Lucien blocked the talons of an attacking demoness with his sword, and then dug his feet into the sand and shoved, managing to push her back enough to get clear. He whirled to parry another deadly thrust of those terrifying claws. *He won't be able to maintain this forever*, Annie realized. Lilith had the advantages of size, strength and outright meanness. *Lucien won't be able to win, but at this close range, the shotgun is more of a liability than a help.* She dropped it to the ground and pulled the .44 Magnum from her hip holster, following the fight from side to side, desperate to get a clear shot. *What did Sarahi say? A headshot, sever the spine, or take out the heart. But all without hitting Lucien.*

Movement across the tableau of a low rise brought her gaze to Josiah. Her beloved stood staring, not at the fight, but at her.

Don't! she urged him silently. *Don't be part of this. Don't take her side. Walk away, Josiah*!

She returned her attention to Lucien. Josiah was doing nothing, so she ignored him.

Lucien rolled to avoid another slash, this one aimed at his throat. The motion brought him directly to Josiah's side. Lucien rose to his feet, looking his son directly in the face. "No matter what happened," he said, "you are my son and I love you."

Then he screamed as Lilith grabbed him from behind, sinking a handful of claws into one side of his back and whirling him around. A slash of her free hand laid open the angel's belly, and blood sprayed across the sand. She threw him to the ground.

"No!" Annie screamed.

Lilith hissed at her and crouched over Lucien, mouth opening wider. Her jaws hyperextending until the lower one rested against her throat, exposing wicked back-curving fangs.

She poised to strike. Annie moved without thought, racing forward at top speed, crouching and slamming into the demoness with her shoulder. The force of her momentum sufficed to knock Lilith off-balance. Quick as a blink, Annie grabbed Lucien in her arms and muttered the words that caused relocation, the only shelter she knew firmly fixed in her mind.

The desert shifted in a rainbow of colors as the demoness pounced onto the exact spot where they had been.

* * *

The world rematerialized into a decomposing bed in the interior of a decrepit trailer. Making a frantic mental plea to Sarahi, Annie ripped off her mask and pressed the fabric into Lucien's belly, trying desperately to staunch the flow of blood and darker fluids. The snowy fabric instantly grew drenched.

"Don't die, Lucien," she begged. "Stay with me." Even as the words crossed her lips, she knew they were useless. *This is not a survivable injury.* The poor angel had been eviscerated, his intestines bulging through the deep slashes in his belly.

Drawing every ounce of strength she possessed, Annie began feeding healing energy into Lucien's wound. *First repair the bowel. The leakage from there could kill on its own.* By the time she had fixed one of the deep gashes, she was exhausted.

"What happened?" The soft voice spoke in her ear. "Oh no!" Sarahi scrambled onto the bed and grasped her husband's hand in hers. "Can you heal him?"

"I tried," Annie said, panting. "It's beyond me. What do I do, Sarahi?"

But Sarahi did not respond, her attention fixed on her husband. "Lucien, love. Hang on. Don't die."

"Let me go, Sarahi," he croaked in an agonized whisper. "I'm done."

"No!" she shouted. "Without you, I have no reason to live. I'll never let you go."

"You have to live, love. You have to keep trying to reach Josiah."

"Wait...Josiah!" Sarahi lifted tear-stained eyes to Annie's face. "Call Josiah!"

"Wha... what?" the girl stammered. "Why?"

"He can give you energy. Only you. Get him here. He can help you," Sarahi babbled.

Annie inhaled an unsteady breath. "How do I call him?"

"The same way you just called me. Hurry!"

Lucien coughed. A trickle of blood streamed from the corner of his mouth.

"Josiah!" Annie screamed. Her voice rang across the desert. Every person heard it, and the battle paused momentarily as warriors from both sides wondered what had happened.

Sarahi took up the cry and sent it, straight as an arrow, into her son's unguarded heart.

Chapter 21

Josiah stood on the battlefield, not participating, only watching. What he had seen so far stunned him. *I grew up around these Nephilim and clerics. I was raised to be one of them. By all rights, I should be fighting alongside them now, but here I am, standing beside a demon.* How had his life gotten so far off track? *Because you're as much demon as angel.*

Mother... he closed his eyes as the image of the beautiful red-haired woman with a sparkling pink aura danced before him. *She gave me up to save me, and that was love. Not perfect, but real. She did the best she could. And Annie, my sweet Annie, who defied her only remaining family to be with me.* Annie's love had sustained him his entire life, and he'd used and abandoned her. *And Father. My stubborn, imperfect, know-it-all father, who endured ten years of silent confinement to be certain I was safe, who's been separated from his beloved for two decades. Father loved me too.*

He'd thrown all that away for this. *For this. I really must be the demon.* Now his father lay wounded, dying somewhere, slain by this woman, this monster he'd chosen to align himself with. He looked at her as she sucked on one long black claw. He shuddered.

Josiah felt sick with grief. Too sick to maintain the shields around his heart that blocked his mother's sweet calls for him to return.

"JOSIAH!" The scream ripped across the desert, and angels and demons alike swiveled, searching for the source. Josiah knew. He knew where it had come from. He knew who was calling him. No one had ever touched him so deeply.

"Josiah," Lilith said, reaching out to him with claws that still dripped his father's blood. He gave her one last look of deep disgust and vanished.

The desert faded into the interior of an ancient, ratty travel trailer. In front of him, on the remains of the bed, Annie sat. The girl glowed with power as she poured her healing energy into his father, who lay on the tattered mattress, inert and bleeding. His mother clutched his father's hand and wept, begging him to hold on.

Sarahi looked up at the sound of his arrival. "Josiah. Oh, thank God. Come on. We need your help!"

He shook his head, not understanding. "What can I do?"

"It's your father," Annie said, "I can't heal him. I need you."

"No," he said. The women blinked at him.

"No?" Annie asked, not believing. "What do you mean, no?"

He shook his head again. "I can't help. I have no gift of healing. What can I do? If I tried, I'd probably just finish him off, and even if I succeeded, I… it wouldn't be any good."

"What are you saying, son?" Sarahi demanded.

"I've done too much. I'm evil now, Mother. Look at me." He trailed his finger through his own aura, highlighting the muddy, gray color. *It has darkened so much.*

"Evil?"

He nodded and forced himself to admit the truth. "I'm a murderer. I killed Peter, and I…"

"I know, son," Sarahi said, her eyes filled with sorrow. "I know. But that doesn't mean you can't help. Please."

"What do you want me to do? I've already told you I don't know how to heal."

"You don't have to," she replied. "Annie has the gift, but she doesn't have enough strength. Give her your power, your energy. She needs it."

"My energy is tainted." He waved at the grayish glow again.

From the bed, Lucien groaned in agony.

"Josiah," Annie said, drawing his eyes to her. "I know you have hard things to face. I get it. But do you really think it will make it easier if you let your father die?"

A shaft of sheer agony pierced Josiah. *If I don't act, Lucien's death, like Peter's, will be on my conscience.* He reached out to Annie through the bonds of love and desire that had bound them since childhood; strengthened in puberty and cemented in his bed a few weeks ago. With a wince of sympathy, he fed his muddy, tainted energy into his beloved. The pure white glow of her aura brightened immediately to a blinding brilliance, like a nuclear blast. Her hands shone like captive stars. She laid her fingers on Lucien's wounded belly. The black skin glowed with an internal luminescence. Annie began to mutter under her breath.

"First repair the lacerations to the bowel." She concentrated. "Good. Now clear contaminants from the belly. No infections." There was a flare of light so bright, it burned against Josiah's retinas like a flash of ignited magnesium. "Repair the muscles. And last the skin...."

Annie released Josiah's energy. It snapped back to him like a rebounding rubber band. He took several steps backwards and ran into the chipped laminate table.

When his vision cleared, he returned his gaze to the scene before him. Annie had risen from the bed and was walking towards him, her gait unsteady, as though she were slightly drunk. Beyond her, his mother had cuddled up against his father's side and pressed her forehead against his cheek. No longer groaning, Lucien had wrapped his arms around her, holding her close. They murmured unintelligible words to each other. Josiah felt a pang of envy. *They're so sweet together, so very connected. I wonder if I'll ever be blessed with what they have.* His gaze returned to Annie. *I want that kind of relationship with her, but I don't deserve it.* Despair quickly turned to rage.

"I'm so glad you came," she said softly. "I'm so glad you returned to us."

"Who says I've returned?" he demanded belligerently.

"What?" Annie looked at him, confused. It seemed he could do nothing other than confound her. "You can't be serious. That bitch is the one who did this!" She gestured behind her at the bed. "She nearly killed him. You can't be planning to return to her."

"Well, no," Josiah admitted. "I won't do that. But it doesn't mean I'm going to fight for the clerics either."

"Why not?"

"Why would I? What have they ever done for me? Annie, you saw what they did. They made my every waking minute miserable. What possible allegiance do I owe them?"

She took another step, close enough to touch him. But she didn't; she only pinned him with those irresistible brown eyes and spoke softly. "You have a point. I won't deny it. The clerics did not do right by you, from my grandfather right down the line to Peter. I would hardly expect you to be loyal to them. But what about to us, Josiah? Look around this room. Everyone here loves you, has always loved you. Don't you owe us your loyalty? If Lilith wins this fight, being disemboweled will be the least we'll face."

Josiah shook his head in confusion. "You, Annie? Why would she go after you?"

"Don't be stupid, Josiah. I was your first lover. Your unlimited energy, the thing she covets so much, belongs to me. Only I can share it, and that fact alone will earn me a terrible death. And there are... other reasons."

Josiah lowered his gaze, trying to figure out what she meant. He studied the line of her body and was startled to see how bright her aura glowed around her belly. He met her eyes again, understanding blossoming.

"I don't deserve you," he said sadly.

"You don't," she agreed. "And I intend to make you suffer and grovel for a long time... *after* the battle."

"I can't believe it. I should take you far away from here. Hide you."

Annie pulled her gun from her belt and waved it casually in his direction. "Try it," she challenged.

"You wouldn't shoot me," he said. *I hope she wouldn't.*

"No," she agreed. "But I'd happily pistol-whip you into the new millennium. Don't give me a reason."

He nodded. "Tough chick," he said tenderly.

"Damn straight, boy. Now get your ass out there and help us fight."

* * *

Lilith stepped forward to the shifting edge of the battle, where a Naphil and a drone were locked together in a bone-crushing fistfight. She couldn't get a clear shot, so she raked her claws across both of them. The drone immediately decomposed into dust, confirming he had been an old one. The Naphil howled until she cut off his scream by biting out his throat. She spat the mouthful of flesh onto the ground in disgust. *He tasted bad. That Lucien, on the other hand, was awfully yummy. No wonder my faithless daughter was been drawn to him.* She strode forward. A Succubus stumbled, knocked aside by a heavy blow from a cleric. Lilith slashed her claws, severing the man's spine and leaving him twitching on the ground. Her daughter stared at her in wide-eyed horror.

"You're welcome," she told the Succubus. The girl turned and fled, leaving Lilith shaking her head. *What a bunch of weak, useless creatures I birthed.* Nearly half had defected, taking their drones with them. Between that and the heavy losses they'd suffered, the armies were now equally matched. *Soon I will have to step in more directly, because I have no intention of losing this fight. Those ridiculous half-angels and their friends will learn the cost of baiting the Queen of Demons.*

A surprising sight, accompanied by a familiar scent, captured her attention. At the edge of the battlefield, near a weathered mesquite tree, an old black man stood, watching the battle and muttering. She stalked over to him and recognized him from many years past. A wicked, rage-filled smile curled her lips, revealing her fangs to the hot desert breeze. "Hello there, Moses," she said, smirking when he jumped, eyes huge. "Did you forget me?"

He shook his head. "Of course not."

"How is your daughter?"

He gulped, taking a deep breath before responding. "She's dead. You know that. Your... firstborn killed her, along with her husband and son."

"Ah, yes. My dear, loyal Jezebel. She's here, now, on this battlefield. Did you know?"

"I guessed." He muttered under his breath something that sounded distinctly like, "That bitch."

Lilith continued in a sultry drawl. "What I've always wondered, Moses, is how you got away from me. I've never had a drone escape. I thought I would be able to keep you."

He shook his head. "I woke up one day and realized I had a choice. I knew what would happen to me if I stayed. I wanted a better life, a real life, so I left. That's all."

She drew close, trailing claws over the front of his shirt. "Did you ever miss me?"

He sneered, retreating several steps. "You're a disgusting creature. My poor late wife, the mother of my daughter, was a hundred times better than you could ever hope to be."

Lilith laughed. "Trying to earn yourself a quick death, Moses? Keep dreaming. I plan to enjoy every moment of my revenge when this little skirmish is over."

With that, she tossed out a net of energy that pinned him against the weathered tree trunk. "There," she said, tying off the knot. "Now you can't sneak away from me again. Be back later, darling." She blew him a kiss and stalked back to the fighting.

Until this day, the abdication of Moses Smith had been her greatest, most humiliating, most devastating loss. *He will pay for it with centuries of agony.* She could keep him alive to suffer at her hands indefinitely. Knowing he wouldn't be able to escape, she considered the remaining fighters, trying to decide who to kill next.

A petite, red-haired figure stepped in front of her. "Hello, Mother."

Lilith raised her eyebrows. "Sarahi? I didn't expect to see you here."

"You should have expected it. You tried to kill my husband."

"Tried?" She laughed. "I did kill him. He may not realize it yet, but there's no coming back from a wound like that. I don't blame you for going to him, though. He was delicious." She licked one of her claws with a long stroke of her forked tongue. Sarahi hissed in fury.

Her own pale pink nails lengthened into rigid spikes. Fangs extended past her lips.

"Come on, you useless lump of flesh. Let's get this over with." Lilith slashed out fast, but Sarahi dodged. Lilith blinked, unused to her daughters avoiding her blows. Even a killing blow. "Stop that, you twit. If you fight me, I'll only kill you slower."

"No," Sarahi replied coolly, "you cannot have my husband. You cannot have my son. I'll fight for them both."

Lilith shrugged. "You can fight, but you'll lose."

She struck out again, cobra fast, and again connected with empty air. "Quit squirming, slut."

"I'm not the slut here, Mother." Sarahi slashed with her own claws and managed to open a wound on her mother's arm. Lilith stared at the blood in amazement. *No one has attacked me directly in millennia, not until today, and now twice in as many hours, and one my own daughter. How remarkable... and infuriating. This time, I won't miss.* She aimed a powerful blow at the little demoness's throat but was brought to a shuddering halt as her claws snared against steel. Lucien stood tall and strong, his obsidian body a silhouette against the low afternoon sun as he blocked her.

"You," she hissed. "I killed you!"

"Apparently not," Lucien said. "I feel fine. But I do need to have a word with you about my son."

"Hmm," Lilith moaned in a parody of ecstasy. "He was goooood. Who would have guessed an angel would be so... skilled?"

Sharp pain stung in her leg. While she'd been distracted by the Naphil, Sarahi had attacked again, attempting to hamstring her. She kicked out, sending the Succubus tumbling. Then she turned her attack to Lucien, driving him back with a lightning-quick series of slashes and jabs. He slowly gave ground, step by step, not engaging, just protecting himself from injury.

He stumbled, going down hard on the hot sand, and Lilith pounced on him in a heartbeat, her fangs extending. *This time I'll tear out his angel throat.*

She gagged as something sharp embedded in the inside of her wide-open mouth. Reaching in, she pulled out a steel throwing star. Scanning with narrowed eyes, she saw that same white-clad figure who'd interfered with this kill before. This time, though, the mask was gone, revealing the pretty face of a girl. *There's something strange about the taste of the young woman's energy. It tastes like...* She flicked her tongue into the air. *It tastes like Josiah.* Lilith ground her teeth in rage. *This is the one, the one who stole my prize.* Another star flew at Lilith, and she dodged.

Once again, she'd forgotten Sarahi. The intrepid Succubus rushed her mother from behind, sinking claws into her back and digging for her spine. Lilith roared and pulled her daughter off her, throwing her across the desert, before stalking after her.

A tall figure approached the fallen Succubus and helped her to her feet.

"Josiah," Lilith hissed, "get away from her."

"She's my mother," he gritted out between his teeth.

What did Jezebel say? Ah, yes, that I should remind him why his life with me is better. "She abandoned you as an infant," Lilith replied. "She deserves nothing from you. None of them do. They all hated and feared you for what you are. They never let you be yourself. Only I did."

Josiah scoffed. "You let me wallow in my basest urges. That's not love, it's temptation. I want no more of it."

"I didn't force it on you, you sought me out. It was what you wanted!" she insisted.

"It was," he agreed, "but it isn't anymore. Annie!"

As Lilith watched, a cord of cloudy, steel-gray energy shot past her. She turned, seeing it connect to the white-clad girl, who lit up like the sun. In the purity of her diamond-clean aura, the dirty-looking energy turned to pure silver.

"Lucien," Annie called, shooting a bolt of it to the Naphil, who caught it in one outstretched hand. He illuminated like a thin shard of obsidian in front of a floodlight.

"Sarahi," Lucien shouted. Lilith whirled and saw her daughter begin to sparkle like a chunk of rose quartz in sunlight. The delicate Succubus seemed taller and stronger.

"Never come between a mother and her child," Sarahi said, holding her claws out threateningly, as she stood between her son and the demon who had given birth to her.

Lilith surged forward across the sand, ready to tear her daughter limb from limb. She reached out both hands and grasped... nothing. Sarahi had dodged her again, rolling to the side. Lilith turned, following the movement, determined to rid herself of her long-standing mistake once and for all. Sarahi surged to her feet and Lilith struck out, but the angle was wrong. The girl had rushed her, and instead of sinking claws into Sarahi's unguarded belly, she only managed to knock her off her feet. Lilith drew her arm back, preparing to finish the job, but she was distracted once again. A sharp pain flared in her back. In her rage, she had forgotten about Lucien. The angel had circled behind her and driven his sword into her spine. She roared, a hissing shriek that sounded like steam escaping from a kettle. Another stab and Lilith doubled over against excruciating pain in her abdomen. Sarahi had risen to her knees and sunk her claws upwards into the demoness's belly, scrabbling behind her ribs, trying to reach her heart. A strange buzzing, like a hive full of bees, sounded in her ears; the thoughts of her daughters and her drones, all chattering and murmuring at the same time.

Another movement snared Lilith's vision. Before her, that damned girl stood watching her. Brown eyes glittered, cold and merciless as topaz in the desert sunset as she raised a pistol, pointing it directly at Lilith's skull from close range.

She saw rather than heard the full lips form the words "Josiah is mine," and then she watched the finger squeeze the trigger. A white light flashed, and Lilith's black aura closed in on her, covering the world in darkness.

Chapter 22

From his position trapped against the trunk of the scrubby tree, Moses Smith watched the desperate fight between his former mistress and his family. The four of them worked in tandem, sharing their strength. Though Lilith's defeat should have been impossible, Lucien severed her spine from behind as Sarahi pulled out a throbbing morsel of flesh, which she clutched in blood-soaked fingers. At that very second, his own precious granddaughter finished the job with a perfect headshot. Unable to overcome the three mortal injuries, the demoness exploded. Whereas her Succubi burst into golden dust, Lilith's combustion resembled the force of a volcanic eruption, and the detritus of the blast—oily black ash—showered over the battlefield. Stunned by the destruction of their leader, the Succubi fled. Drones stumbled after them, leaving their wounded and dead among the surviving Nephilim and Clerics. *The battle is over. The powers of light have won.*

Moses watched awareness dawn on the faces of the men he had known and led. As one they began cheering, hugging one another and jumping up and down in delight. He smiled. *But why am still trapped? Why has Lilith's energy net not dispersed with her death? No matter. Someone will find me soon enough. For now, I'm content to watch.* The bonds of energy that connected Naphil, Succubus, Incubus, and Assassin winked out and Sarahi collapsed to the ground. The poor girl had taken the brunt of the blast, being so close to Lilith when she was destroyed. Lucien also crumpled slowly onto his back. Further away, Annie and Josiah staggered but managed to keep their feet. They stood motionless for a long moment before running to one another. The boy caught her up and twirled her around, crushing her in his arms and kissing her. Then, hand in hand, they approached the prone figures of Josiah's parents. The light flared around the younger couple and

Annie knelt, laying her hand on Lucien's chest. After a brief surge of light, he took a deep breath and sat up. Annie moved on to Sarahi, pulsing healing energy into Josiah's mother. She stirred but didn't wake. Annie pulsed her energy a second time and drew back, shaking her head. Lucien scooted over to his wife and gathered her into his arms. *No one seems hysterical, so she probably isn't dead, but she's clearly still unconscious.*

Annie and Josiah knelt, hugging Lucien briefly before rising to walk across the battlefield. Time and again Annie knelt, sending pulses of energy into prone figures. Some sat up. Some stirred. Others remained still. Not every wound could be healed, even with the combined efforts of a healer and an Incubus. To one side, the black-haired Succubus Salome relished an indiscreet embrace with her husband. Her Naphil had backed her up against a scraggly tree trunk and was ravishing her mouth with one wild kiss after another. Moses shook his head and returned to watching Annie and her beloved as they continued to travel across the blasted desert, healing friend and foe alike. At last, they circled around to his vicinity.

"Annie," he called.

"Grandfather?"

"Yes, I'm over here. Come help, please."

She approached, holding Josiah's hand. When the young man saw him, the cat green eyes narrowed to glowing slits. He released Annie and stalked forward, his dirty-looking aura flickering to life. A blade of pure energy shone in his grasp.

"Josiah," Annie scolded, "what are you doing?"

"Taking care of unfinished business," the boy replied.

Moses's heart began to beat faster. *He's as dangerous as Lilith, and it's just as personal.* "He's going to finish me, girl. That's why I never wanted you with him. I knew what he was, even before I found out about his demon blood. He's a killer by nature, like his grandmother."

"Josiah," Annie said, clearly trying to catch the young man's attention. "Josiah, come on. Don't do anything stupid."

"Stupid?" Amusement twisted the tan face into a grim smile, complete with flashing white teeth. "Stupid to exact justice on the man who has tormented me since I was a child? A grown man, Annie, bullying a little boy. How was that right? If I'm a demon, he's the one who made me one, with all his ugly talk and two-faced judgmental attitudes. Lilith didn't make me a monster; I never knew her. If I have hatred, bitterness, despair and death in my soul, it is not because of my demon blood. It is because of this man. How can you deny me justice? How can you deny it *is* justice?"

"I don't," Annie said, making Moses gape. "He never acted right where you were concerned. It was a travesty. But please, Josiah. Don't kill my grandfather. Don't take another life. Please, show mercy."

" 'I will show mercy on whom I will show mercy,' " the boy quoted. " 'And I will pardon whom I will pardon.' "

"Stop it," Annie wailed. "You're not God."

"I am to him. Here, in this moment, I am." He turned to look at her and she fell silent.

"Go on then, boy," Moses taunted. "Be the demon you are. Finish me. Do it."

Josiah smiled again, and there was death in that smile. The blade of energy flashed, and Moses flinched, but he managed to restrain the scream welling up inside him. *I will die like a man.*

Only he didn't die. The crushing net of energy that had held him captive fell away and dissipated. He was free, and Josiah had cut the cord.

Moses blinked in surprise. "Why?" he asked.

"Demon is a choice," Josiah replied. "If I don't act like one, I'm not one. Do you know who taught me that, old man? My half-demon mother. And do you want to know something else?"

"What," Moses asked warily.

"I forgive you." Josiah released his hold on his energy and walked away leaving Moses to consider what had just happened in speechless astonishment.

Chapter 23

"Is she going to be all right?" Lucien asked, his voice gravelly with emotion. He watched the medic, a distinguished-looking man with silver at his temples and a neatly-clipped goatee, pressing gently on Sarahi's belly. She lay in a bed in the infirmary of the compound, still unconscious.

"There's some swelling here. I think there may have been some internal bleeding at one point, but it doesn't seem life-threatening. What happened?"

"She got too close to the explosion."

"Ah," said a nurse, lifting a fragment of oily black goo from Sarahi's chin. "That explains this."

Lucien nodded. "Annie healed her... or at least tried to, but she wasn't able to complete the process."

"I suppose," the medic replied, "being part demon, their energy wasn't compatible. At least she repaired the injury. Internal bleeding can be very dangerous. She also has a concussion, though it doesn't seem too serious. She'll wake up with a monster of a headache."

Lucien stroked a strand of rumpled burgundy hair from her forehead. "It could have been worse."

"Yes, much worse," the nurse agreed.

Lucien sat by while the team continued to work on her, administering anti-swelling medication, icing the bump on her head, cleaning and bandaging her multiple abrasions, and washing the blood from her skin.

"What *is* this?" asked the nurse, scraping ugly globs out from under her fingernails.

"Don't ask," Lucien replied. *I don't want to explain little bits of Lilith.*

"Father?" Lucien looked up to see Josiah, his hair still wet from a shower, standing hesitantly in the doorway.

"Josiah," he replied, not knowing what else to say.

"Is she all right?"

Lucien turned to the medic.

"With rest and time, she should be fine."

Josiah nodded. "Can I come in?"

"She's your mother," Lucien said. "Of course, you can."

Josiah pulled up a chair and sat down. He took Sarahi's limp, freshly cleaned hand in his. He gulped and drew in a shaky-sounding breath. "This is my fault."

Lucien considered his words. "No, this war has been coming since the dawn of time. You were the catalyst, nothing more."

"'Things that cause people to stumble are bound to come, but woe to anyone through whom they come. It would be better for them to be thrown into the sea with a millstone tied around their neck.'" Josiah quoted, his eyes cast down.

"Don't overdo it, son," Lucien urged. "We won, after all. If you caused the battle, you're responsible for the victory, and I think you've suffered plenty for your rebellion, haven't you?"

"Yes." Josiah said nothing more, but the expression on his face told Lucien everything he needed to know.

"Anything can be forgiven if there is true repentance," he said.

"Anything?" Josiah burst out in a torrent of self-flagellation. "I almost got my mother killed. I got my girlfriend pregnant and then slept with another woman." He made a small, involuntary movement as though suppressing a gag. "I lived with demons for weeks, and by not acting against their behavior, I condoned it. And I murdered Peter. Can I really come back from that? Will you forgive me? Will Mom? Will Annie?" His voice grew soft, almost a whisper. "Will I ever forgive myself?"

"I can," Lucien promised, "and I know your mother will. As for Annie... well, I suspect you'll have to grovel for a while, but she's loved you forever, Josiah. Give her a little time. I think she'll be okay eventually, especially since you're back."

The last question he did not address. It's too soon. *I don't know what it will take for Josiah to forgive himself, but I suspect a lot of effort and time will be needed.* In the meanwhile, the boy could sit beside his mother, stroke her hand, and think about how to make the future better than the past.

* * *

"Argh," Sarahi groaned as the light in the infirmary switched on. She turned, hiding her face against Lucien's leg. Despite the weeks that had passed since the battle, she still suffered from blinding headaches and light sensitivity. The pain made her nauseous.

"Sorry," the nurse said to her, and then, to someone else, "What's wrong, hon?"

"I don't know. I suddenly feel hungry all the time. Poor Caleb can't keep up," Sarahi heard her kindest sister say.

"Well I don't know very much about Succubus anatomy but let me take a look."

Sarahi smiled through the pain. *I know exactly what's troubling Salome.*

* * *

So, Salome is pregnant, Lucien thought as he walked down the hallway from the courtyard back to the apartment he shared with his wife... or used to share. It had been weeks since the battle. *Sarahi is happy for her sister, of course, but one setback after another has kept her trapped in the infirmary.*

The black-haired beauty, on the other hand, glowed with radiant joy, and Annie was starting to show a little. *She hasn't consented to marry Josiah yet, but I suspect she will. She's just making him squirm as punishment for his sins before she agrees. I don't disapprove. My son has a lot of atoning to do to a lot of people.*

My wife. His thoughts cycled back to Sarahi, still lying on that infirmary bed. *If only I could slip in between the sheets and take her in his arms. I'll be so gentle as I feed her back to health. The nurses simply can't grasp the concept, and keep chasing me away, but soon I'll have to be forthright with them no matter how uncomfortable it is. Maybe tomorrow. Yes, that will be good. I'll get a good night's sleep, eat a hearty breakfast, and then absolutely insist on some privacy so I can heal my wife. We both need it.*

He arrived at their bedroom, opened the door and froze in astonishment.

* * *

Annie stood in the courtyard, clad in a warm, fur-lined jacket, looking up at the stars. The January air bit at her cheeks and gnawed her nose, though no wind blew. Her fingers ached inside her mittens and she tucked them into her pockets.

A warm body pressed against her back, arms wrapping around her. "Hello, beautiful," a deep voice whispered in her ear.

"Josiah," she said, struggling to sound neutral.

"Can we talk, Anne?"

"I'm not doing anything. Talk."

"I'm sorry."

"I forgive you." She still sounded flat, she knew, but she feared opening up the floodgate of confused emotions Josiah evoked in her. She hated that their relationship had become so complicated. He kissed her cheek. The pleasure of his warm lips on her cold face retained its simplicity. It still felt perfect.

"Talk to me, Annie, please."

"About what, Josiah?"

"About what I can do. I love you. I've always loved you. I know I screwed up. I made a terrible mess out of every good thing we had. Is there any way I can make it right? Just say the word. If you want a star to keep in your pocket, I'll find a way. Please, Annie. How can I make this better?"

"I don't know, Josiah. I just don't know. Did you really..."

His forehead dropped onto her shoulder. "Yes."

"But she was your..."

"I know. It was stupid. I hated it the moment it was finished. But by then it was too late."

"Then why? Why did you... do that? Wasn't my love enough for you? Why did you run from my bed to hers?"

"Your love was enough for me. More than enough. That was the most perfect moment of my entire life. The first thing that had ever felt so right. But...Annie, a few hours later, I was ready to fight heaven and earth to have you. And then I found out I was a demon. That my grandmother was our ultimate enemy. That my own mother was a Succubus. How could I inflict that on my perfect Annie? My shining star? That's why I left. Not because I loved you too little, but because I loved you too much.

"That's the Othello excuse," Annie said. "It didn't hold water with him murdering his wife, and it doesn't hold water with you... doing what you did."

"It doesn't. There is no excuse, and I don't want to give one. I can't undo the past, Annie. I deserve you less than ever. But I've made peace with what I am. If Mother can risk her life against one of the greatest evils the world has ever known, how can I use demon blood as an excuse? I can't. I won't. I am what I am, Annie. You knew it, and you loved me anyway. I'm grateful for that. I don't know if you can love me again, knowing the choices I've made. If not, it's no less than I deserve. It would be justice if you found another man to love you. But this is mine, my doing." His hand cupped the tiny swell of her belly. "My child. I grew up without parents for half my childhood, Annie, and I don't want that for our baby. Can you let me try? Can you let it go enough for me at least to be part of our baby's life? Please, Annie?"

He's begging. Annie closed her eyes against the sting of tears. Josiah was begging her to forgive him. For what reason was she withholding it? He was suffering, she knew. Part of her wanted his pain, took grim satisfaction in it. But most of her wanted him in her arms every day, in her bed every night. And then an image of her beloved servicing that disgusting demon flashed in her mind.

"Josiah, maybe we should... talk to someone about everything that's happened. A counselor? One of the elders? Someone who can help us both come to terms with life as it exists now?"

"Do I dare to hope that might be pre-marital counseling?" He kissed her cheek again.

"No," she replied, and felt his body sag in defeat. She turned, wrapping her arms around his neck. "Post-marital. I want to get married tomorrow."

She watched the understanding dawn in his eyes. Then he lowered his face, touching his lips to hers in a tender, passionate kiss.

* * *

"Hello, Lucien," Sarahi said to her startled husband. Lucien just stared. Why was she here, in their bed, waiting for him? Why was she not languishing in the infirmary?

"Sarahi?" he said. When he was able to focus on the scene, he noticed a Succubus intent on seduction knew how to make a compelling presentation. The bed was made up with a black satin comforter, pulled back to reveal scarlet sheets. She sat on the colorful fabric, wearing a clinging black lace nightgown which revealed more than it concealed of her luscious figure. Her full breasts strained the fabric to the breaking point. It skimmed her pale, narrow waist and the little curve of her belly before flaring across her lush hips, to her soft thighs. Her long red hair spilled around her shoulders and down her back. His eyes went back to her belly. It was small now, just part of her curves, but he had never forgotten how beautiful she'd looked, swollen with his child. He'd doted on her during her pregnancy, more than ever, knowing the blessing for what it was. *We can try again*, he thought. *Have another child. One we will raise together as husband and wife.*

But first, he would have to plant a baby in her. And in order to do so, he would have to help her get well. Even now she looked pale and strained. There were lines of tension around her mouth, as though she were still in pain. Her eyes also showed the strain, the emerald depths dimmed.

"How did you get here, love? How did you set all this up?"

"Salome helped me," she replied. "She told the nurse I needed you if I wanted to get well. She brought me here and made up the bed. I didn't do anything but get dressed. But I want you now. I need you. Come to me, my love."

Lucien had no intention of arguing. Despite appearing as fragile as a porcelain doll, which made his protective instincts want to tuck her into bed, he knew she needed his loving in order to regain her strength. Sitting beside her on the bed, he took her in his arms and kissed her, a long and lingering kiss. She cupped his face and held him still while she covered his lips with endless, clinging kisses. She drank hungrily of his mouth, and he could feel copious amounts of energy pouring into her damaged body. He held nothing back from his lady. Nothing. He fed his life force into her, preparing her for the even more sustaining meal to come. She pulled his sweater over his head, and he returned the favor, divesting her of the lace negligée and laying her back on the bed, spreading her hair across the pillow. Such a compelling picture she made; black and white and red, with the glow of her eyes for contrast. He straddled her hips and kissed her again before moving to the tempting globes of her breasts. He stroked and caressed one while capturing the rosy nipple of the other in his teeth, lashing it with his tongue and then sucking hard.

Sarahi moaned and tossed her head against the pillow as he worked the sensitive peak.

"Over here, love," she urged, guiding his mouth to the other breast where it seemed the nipple begged for his attention. He gave it. She stroked his hair as he pleasured her. He kissed his way down her belly to the sweet, wet cleft of her body. He wanted to taste her and, using his fingers to spread her folds apart, he kissed her there before devastating his lady with long, tender licks. He worked her feminine flesh, bringing her to the peak of ecstasy. She didn't have the strength to come hard, but moisture surged against his lips. She was ready for her man, and he was more than ready for her. Kneeling between her thighs, he aligned his aching sex with her ready passage and slipped gently inside her, sliding deep into her waiting body.

"Ooh," she sighed. Then she sobbed softly as Lucien pulled back and pressed in again, setting up a slow rhythm. Every time he pressed forward, energy poured from him into her. Her cheeks flushed with pleasure. Seeing she was stronger, he grasped her hips and thrust harder. Her breath caught. A moment later she was writhing in pleasure, whimpering and clawing at his back.

Remembering those claws, he grabbed her arms and pinned them to the bed above his head as he gave her his last few strokes and poured his seed into her welcoming body.

After giving away so much energy, Lucien collapsed on Sarahi. She slipped her hands out from under his and embraced him.

"Are you all right, darling?"

"Not a problem," he sighed. "You?"

"All better. You healed me. I didn't take too much, did I?"

"No. I'll need a good night's sleep, and a huge breakfast, but I'll be fine. I love you, Sarahi."

"And I love you, Lucien. Can you believe we survived? That we won?

"I know. It's amazing. I also can't believe I'm still awake." He yawned hugely and rolled to his side, pulling her close.

Epilogue

Josiah married Annie the next day, and eventually, the couple did come to terms with all that had happened. Their son was later joined by two daughters.

The Nephilim continued protecting humanity from rogue Succubi. But without the influence of Lilith, the work was both easier and safer.

In the autumn, Lucien and Sarahi welcomed a tiny, brown-eyed daughter to their family. Lucien quipped at the delivery that after everything they had faced, how much trouble could one little baby be? He soon found out.

And so, the angel and the demon found a way to live together, not only in peace but in joy. And so, the prophecies of the Succubi, the Nephilim, and the one who was called the Incubus came true, just as had been foretold, and the will of Heaven was maintained.

Dear reader,

We hope you enjoyed reading *The Naphil's Kiss.* Please take a moment to leave a review, even if it's a short one. Your opinion is important to us.

Discover more books by Simone Beaudelaire at https://www.nextchapter.pub/authors/simone-beaudelaire-romance-author

Want to know when one of our books is free or discounted? Join the newsletter at http://eepurl.com/bqqB3H

Best regards,

Simone Beaudelaire and the Next Chapter Team

You could also like:

Sisterhood of Fear by Simone Beaudelaire

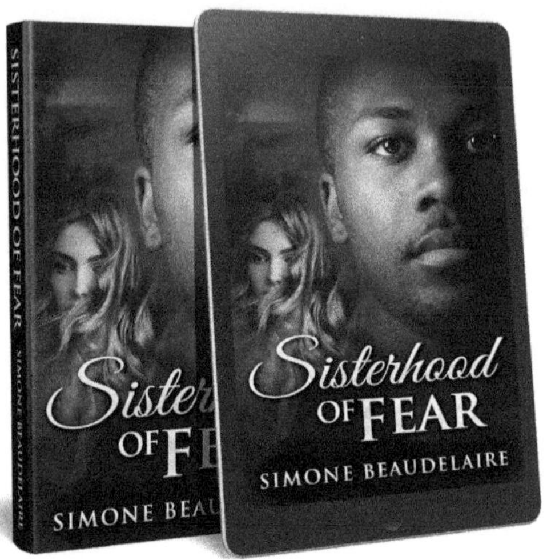

To read the first chapter for free, please head to:
https://www.nextchapter.pub/books/sisterhood-of-fear

The Naphil's Kiss
ISBN: 978-4-86747-554-6

Published by
Next Chapter
1-60-20 Minami-Otsuka
170-0005 Toshima-Ku, Tokyo
+818035793528
28th May 2021

Lightning Source UK Ltd.
Milton Keynes UK
UKHW041924150621
385583UK00001B/102

9 784867 475546